IT ALL STARTED WITH A KISS . . .

SHE SAID:

Tim traced her lips with his thumb as Meg stared into his eyes, mesmerized. "You're very beautiful, Megan Henry," he whispered. Slowly, Tim bent his head until his lips were just inches from hers.

"Do I seem like one of your modern anti-heroes?" he asked quietly. "Am I dangerous, confused, angst-ridden?" His soft voice sent shivers up her spine.

She shook her head slowly. "You may be more dangerous than you realize," she whispered.

"Let's hope so, for both our sakes."

Then he kissed her.

HE SAID:

"I had an amazing time, too," he heard her say. Why was it that every time she spoke he was so mesmerized by her eyes that he couldn't concentrate on her words?

Tim decided the solution was to stop talking and take action. He pushed Meg gently against the wooden fence behind them and bent his head so that his lips were just an inch from hers. Moments later, she closed the space. Her lips were soft and warm under his, and Tim had the sensation that he was floating on a cloud.

As he closed his eyes and pressed his body more tightly against hers, a surprising thought flashed across his mind: Kissing someone had never felt this right.

Dear Reader:

Just a moment of your time could earn you $1,000! We're working hard to bring you the best books, and to continue to do that we need your help. Simply turn to the back of this book, and let us know what you think by answering seven important questions.

Return the completed survey with your name and address filled in, and you will automatically be entered in a drawing to win $1,000, subject to the official rules.

Good luck!

Geoff Hannell

Geoff Hannell
Publisher

Part I
SHE SAID

To Mindy Sue Schultz—and her one true love

The Truth About Love

One

Megan Henry sat cross-legged on her bed, gazing at the zippered clear plastic bag that held the dress she would wear in just a few hours. On her varnished pine dresser were the sparkling rhinestone earrings and bracelet she'd borrowed from her mother.

"Tonight the old Megan Henry is going to stay home and watch TV while the new Megan Henry mingles with dozens of sophisticated college graduates," Meg announced to her best friend, Gretchen Rubin, on the telephone.

"Weddings are so romantic." Gretchen sighed. "I read somewhere that thirty percent of all married couples met at a friend's wedding."

"Wow. That means I have a one-in-three chance of meeting Mr. Wonderful tonight."

"You're so lucky. How many fifteen-year-olds get to be a bridesmaid in their beautiful cousin's wedding,

3

marching down the aisle in a dusty-rose floor-length gown while hundreds of eyes watch admiringly?"

Meg smiled at Gretchen's romantic description of the night ahead. Unfolding her long, thin legs, Meg stood up, still cradling the phone to her ear. She walked over to her full-length mirror and studied her reflection. "Gretchen, you should be a poet," she said with a laugh. "But you're right. I am lucky. And Caroline is luckier. She's marrying Rick, going on a honeymoon, and moving into her own house. No more parents and no more rules." She sighed dramatically. "But when the wedding is over I'm still going to be stuck in my boring high school life, with boring high school boys and boring high school friends—present company excluded."

"Well, the present company is having a psychic premonition that you're going to catch the wedding bouquet and be swept off your feet by a handsome stranger."

Meg made a face at the mirror, lifting one eyebrow and pouting her lips in a way she hoped was sexy and glamorous. "Tim Wilson is going to be at the wedding," she said.

Gretchen groaned. "You're not still infatuated with him, are you? Meg, he's a freshman in college and the star of his soccer team, not to mention gorgeous. Face facts—he is undeniably and categorically out of your league. I was thinking of a handsome stranger along the lines of Billy Jenkins."

Meg grinned. "Billy Jenkins doesn't exactly qualify as a stranger."

"No, but he did just break up with his girlfriend, Patricia Hamlon, the senior who should be voted most likely to be hit by a Mack truck—because her nose is stuck so high in the air she wouldn't be able to see the truck coming."

Batting her eyelashes in the mirror, Meg thought about Billy. True, he was probably the best-looking guy in school, and a junior. She'd had a crush on him since she was in the eighth grade. But it was Tim Wilson who made her heart pound.

Meg had gone to some of the college soccer games with her cousin, Caroline, whose fiancé was the assistant coach. She loved watching Tim's sculpted, muscular legs as he ran down the field. After the game, he would be surrounded by girls who couldn't wait to offer their congratulations and tell him how great he was. Meg had never worked up the nerve to say anything to him, and Tim hadn't even noticed she was alive.

When Meg didn't respond, Gretchen continued. "You know, I'm probably going to see Billy tonight. I heard a lot of juniors are going to be at Michael Levy's barbecue."

"Gretchen, Gretchen, Gretchen. You go ahead and enjoy yourself ogling the junior guys. As far as I'm concerned, they're old news. Between sixth grade and now, I've dated enough of the guys in our school to know that one isn't much different from another. They may come in different shapes and sizes, but they're all just a bunch of hormones in overdrive. Tonight I'm yearning for something different—really different. Who knows, maybe on the way to Caroline's I'll meet a genie. If I do, my first wish will be that the old Meg Henry evaporate into a thin mist, often remembered but never seen again."

• • •

Late Saturday afternoon, Meg sat in her cousin's bedroom, waiting for the five other bridesmaids to finish getting dressed and help her with her hair and makeup. Outside, the late April air was warm and breezy. *I'm glad Caroline decided to get married at home,* Meg thought. The big Victorian house was right out of a nineteenth-century novel, complete with a sprawling back lawn and a circular driveway. From the open bedroom window, Meg watched the caterers preparing the food and setting the tables. She had never been to such a fancy party, and she could hardly wait to float across the lawn in her new high heels, sampling appetizers and carrying a champagne glass filled with sparkling cider.

Meg spotted her mother next to the back door, laughing with Meg's aunt Judy. As Judy hurried off to see about getting extra chairs, Meg's mother glanced up and spotted Meg watching her. She waved and blew her daughter a kiss. Meg sighed. She knew she should be grateful to have such a great mom. In her early forties, Ellen Henry was still fun and spontaneous. She was always patient with her only child, and tried to treat Meg like a real person, not just an annoying, ill-mannered teenager. And Meg's father, Matthew, was equally good-natured. Gretchen even thought that Mr. Henry was attractive. Whenever he came into the room, Gretchen would blush and forget what she was talking about.

But lately Meg could hardly stand to be in the same room with either of her parents for more than five minutes. They were always asking her where she'd been or where she was going. They wanted to know what grade she'd received on her Algebra II test, or whether she'd gotten a head start on the research for her history paper on Lorenzo de Medici. Although Meg had always been a top student, of late she didn't care about Lorenzo de Medici or the English Restoration or how to conjugate the French verb *être* in the subjunctive. She wanted to read novels about the open road; she could see herself in a black leather jacket speeding down the highway on a motorcycle, the wind whipping through her long blond hair. And if that image seemed a little far out, she'd settle for going to mature parties with a great boyfriend—preferably one who didn't think throwing spitballs and having belching contests was an entertaining way to spend an afternoon.

Meg listened to the other bridesmaids' laughter. All in their early twenties, most of the girls had already graduated from college. Meg admired their self-confidence. They weren't even nervous about walking down the aisle with seventy people staring at them in silence.

Caroline's best friend, Gloria Fain, turned to Meg. "We're almost ready to perform surgery on you, Meg. By the time we're done with your makeover, you'll think that awkward adolescence was just a bad dream," Gloria said.

"I can't wait," Meg answered. At Caroline's wedding shower two weeks earlier, Meg had told the girls of her doubts about being in her cousin's wedding. She didn't want the guests to be fussing over her, saying how precious she looked in her grown-up dress.

"Don't worry," Gloria had said. "The night of the wedding, we'll use our powers to turn you into the new Megan Henry. All the guys will be asking who the beautiful girl from out of town is!"

Meg smiled at the memory. She couldn't wait to see the look on her mom's face when she walked out of the house looking like a college woman.

Leaving the older girls to finish getting ready, Meg went in search of Caroline. She found her cousin in the master bedroom, already dressed in her wedding gown. Meg gasped at the sight. Caroline's ivory silk gown was full and long, emphasizing her small waist and barely grazing the hardwood floor of the bedroom. The bodice and short cap sleeves were beaded with shiny seed pearls that twinkled under the overhead light. Meg thought Caroline looked like a vision from a dream. Meg's aunt Judy stood next to her daughter, arranging Caroline's long tulle veil.

"Meg, there you are! I was afraid I wasn't going to see my favorite cousin before the ceremony," Caroline exclaimed.

Judy muttered something about flowers and left the room.

"Should I be ready?" Meg asked, looking down at her jeans and T-shirt in horror.

Caroline laughed. "Don't have a fit. I got dressed early because I have to go have pictures taken with my parents. Ugh! Even on your wedding day, they own you."

Meg was surprised to hear Caroline sounding

like the same girl she'd known all her life. To Meg, her cousin appeared all of a sudden to have become a grown woman.

"Are you nervous?" Meg asked.

"Well, I do have butterflies in my stomach, but they're the good kind. I feel like I just won a huge prize, and I'm on my way to collect it from the officials. Do you know what I mean?"

Meg shook her head.

"Meg, someday you'll feel just like I do now, and I'll come in and find you in your wedding dress. I'll be an old married lady by that point, nodding sagely while you tell me how you feel like your life is about to begin all over again."

"I wish it didn't have to be someday," Meg said. "I want to feel that way now."

Caroline reached over and smoothed Meg's hair away from her forehead. "Just remember that becoming Mrs. Honan doesn't mean I'm not your plain old cousin Caroline anymore. I'll always be there for you."

Meg hugged her cousin gingerly, careful of Caroline's gown and makeup. "Thanks," she whispered. Then she left Caroline to see if it was time for her own promised metamorphosis.

Meg sat at Caroline's dressing table, her eyes closed. The other bridesmaids—Gloria, Maddie, Jessica, Kate, and Laurie—were huddled around her. They'd given her strict instructions not to peek at herself in the mirror before the transformation was absolutely complete. So Meg sat like a mannequin, blind and unmoving, while the older girls argued over styles and colors. But she couldn't keep from smiling. Even though she felt self-conscious, Meg loved the feeling of being in the spotlight, the subject of heated and enthusiastic debate.

"Let's put her hair in a French braid, then loop it under and tie it with a ribbon. And we should use peach tones for her makeup—except for the eyes," Maddie suggested.

"No. I think a simple chignon and a flower behind her ear would be perfect," Kate countered.

"Why don't we give her small curls and pull them back with a gold barrette?" Jessica chimed in. "Mauve colors for the makeup. Peach would wash her out."

"I think a dozen small braids, tied individually with different-colored bows, would be really wild," Laurie said.

"Are all of you crazy?" Gloria asked. "Meg wants to be elegant and sophisticated. She doesn't want to look like some porcelain knickknack on one of our grandmothers' mantelpieces."

Meg sat quietly, enjoying the feel of blush, eyeliner, and mascara being applied to her face. For what seemed like hours she looked up, looked down, pursed her lips, tilted her chin, and did everything else that she was instructed to do.

Finally the bridesmaids stood back to gaze at Meg. "Wow," Kate said. "I can't wait to see her with the dress!"

"We should earn our living doing this," Laurie stated.

"Meg, we owe this all to you. Our collaborative artwork would have ended in disaster if you hadn't

supplied us with the perfect face to express our-
selves on," Gloria said.

"Your cheekbones are practically up to your eyebrows," Maddie observed, sighing. "And we
haven't even mentioned your hair! Get ready to
break a few hearts tonight, Meg."

Meg was giddy with excitement. Being careful
not to look in the mirror, she slipped on her dress
and high heels. With her new sheer pantyhose on,
the shoes felt better than they had when she'd
been walking around her house for practice. Finally
she added her mother's rhinestone jewelry.

Gloria led Meg to a full-length mirror. "Okay. You
can look now," she announced with a flourish.

For the second time that night, Meg gasped. She
couldn't believe it was herself, wide-eyed with
wonder, staring back from the mirror. She
appeared years older, and even her posture was
different. The girl in the mirror was graceful, secure
in her own beauty.

Gloria had swept Meg's ash-blond hair on top of
her head and arranged it in a loose knot. Several
tendrils fell around her heart-shaped face. For her
makeup, Kate had chosen soft pinks, emphasizing
Meg's own coloring, so that the effect was purely
natural. The pinks harmonized with the rose color
of Meg's dress, turning its simple lines into a dramatic statement. And the honey-colored shadow
Laurie had brushed onto Meg's eyelids made her
brown eyes stand out like dark, entrancing pools in
her face.

Meg turned around and around, staring at herself
from every angle. "Will anyone believe it's me?"

"Of course they'll believe it's you, Meg," Gloria answered. "You're always beautiful; it's just that usually your good looks are a little— How should I say it? Well, a little *younger*."

"Thank you all so much," Meg murmured breathlessly. "You can't know how much this means to me. You could never know how much!"

Meg walked down the aisle next to Rick's best man, John Kingsley, in a daze. At rehearsal the day before, she'd been awkward, barely keeping time with the simple rhythm of the wedding march. But that evening every step she took was sure and steady. And the last-minute practicing she'd done with her new high heels had paid off, freeing Meg from the worry that she would wobble or trip while all eyes were glued to the procession.

Meg saw her mother and father twisted around in their seats, beaming at her. She imagined the day that she would walk down the aisle as a bride, full of the love and confidence that she'd seen in Caroline. Maybe she would even wear Caroline's gown. . . .

Meg came out of her reverie when she saw Tim Wilson out of the corner of her eye. In his black tuxedo he was even better-looking than he'd been all the times she'd seen him on the soccer field. His blond hair was shiny and tamed, curling around his ears and down to his collar. When she saw Tim's gaze sweep over her, Meg's heart raced furiously. She could feel herself blush, turning a shade pinker than the color of her dress.

And then Meg found herself at the altar. She stepped aside, and the audience rose from their seats. As Meg turned to watch her cousin walk down the aisle, her eyes moved from Caroline to Tim. With one hand resting on the back of his chair, Tim looked casual and self-assured. Meg willed him to glance in her direction. Suddenly Tim's profile shifted and he was staring directly at her. His eyes rested on her for only a second, but Meg knew that she would experience that moment in slow-motion replay for the entire evening. It was as if someone had stepped into Meg's world and lifted her from the mundane everydayness of her life. The night was a fantasy waiting to happen, and if she could just get Tim Wilson to play the role of her knight in shining armor, Meg could tell Gretchen the story to end all stories.

Waiting for the exchange of vows to begin, Meg thought back to her earlier conversation with Gretchen. *Well, I didn't find a genie, but maybe five bridesmaids are just as good!*

Two

Meg emerged from the trancelike state she'd been in during the ceremony to the sound of her mother's voice. "Honey, you look absolutely beautiful. I was so shocked when I saw you walking down the aisle that I nearly fell out of my seat. For a second I forgot you were a bridesmaid—not the bride!"

Meg hugged her mother. "Thanks, Mom. You know, I think I could get into this wedding thing. Everybody's in a great mood, you get to dress up, and there's catered food afterward!"

"Don't worry. When you're Caroline's age, you'll be going to so many weddings that you'll start thinking champagne and shrimp on a toothpick are daily fare."

Suddenly surrounded by family friends, Meg's mother turned to gush over how moving the wedding had been and what a beautiful bride Caroline was. As she drifted away from the crowd Meg thought about the ceremony. Insisting on a very personal wedding, Caroline and Rick had written their own vows. They reasoned that if marriage was for life, the words of their promise were worth some time and effort.

Meg had gotten goosebumps during the ceremony, and she had them again now, thinking of the solemn vow that Caroline had made to Rick. Her voice soft but firm, Caroline had said that until their marriage, she and Rick had been like two streams traveling alone. But the ceremony signified the joining of their streams into one full river. She'd taken a tiny step closer to Rick when she went on to say that whatever rocks lay in their path, they would always move forward together.

Caroline and Rick had stood eye to eye, and when they exchanged braided gold wedding bands, Meg had felt that the rings were a perfect symbol of their love.

Twilight had darkened into a deep, velvet night, and the spring air fell over Meg's shoulders like a soft shawl. Meg looked up at the stars. Her life of tests, book reports, and the French club seemed eons away; in its place was a world where people never stopped laughing and everyone was lovely.

While the chairs from the wedding ceremony were being whisked away and rearranged around tables for dinner, Meg observed the rest of the guests. Everyone was milling around, greeting one another and searching out the bride and groom to offer quick congratulations. She went over to a table laden with gifts, most wrapped in a variation of the thick silver and white paper Meg had used on her own present to Caroline and Rick.

Meg had worked on her gift for hours, not wanting just to sign her name to the card that Meg's mother had put with the silver pitcher she'd chosen for the newlyweds. Meg's gift was a framed collage of the many photographs of Caroline and Rick that she'd accumulated over the last few years. Under the pictures she'd written captions on colorful pieces of construction paper. Caroline and Rick had loved the present, and Meg had been full of pride when Rick put his arm around her and said, "Well, for my new kid cousin, you're not a bad artist. I think I'll get used to this wacky family after all."

Meg made her way to the table where she knew she was sitting for dinner. All of the tables were under the huge tent that had been erected in the backyard, and each place setting had next to it a hand-painted card with the name of a guest. Earlier Gloria had seen Meg and yelled, "Hey, flower girl, you're sitting with me for dinner. It's the table next to that huge potted plant." On each table was a centerpiece of white and pink roses surrounded by ferns and baby's-breath. And next to everyone's plate was a disposable camera. *Maybe I can sneak a picture of Tim Wilson*, Meg thought. *For that matter, maybe I can get my picture taken with Tim. Now that would be a good memento to show Gretchen!*

Since the ceremony, Meg had caught only brief glimpses of Tim. Each time she'd seen him, he'd been talking to some older person, and Meg hadn't had the guts to try to join in. She hoped she'd have a view of him from her seat. Maybe she could even make some eye contact during dinner. Meg imagined looking up from her plate and catching Tim staring at her from across the lawn. He would smile and raise his wine glass. "To you," he would mouth silently.

Meg saw Kate approach the table, and she quickly pulled her aside.

"Kate, do you know where Tim Wilson is sitting tonight?" Meg asked.

"You mean tall, good-looking Tim with the blond hair and bright blue eyes?"

"Yeah, him."

"You mean star-of-his-soccer-team Tim?"

"*Yes,*" Meg practically shouted.

"Freshman?" Kate teased her.

"Kate, do you know where he's sitting or not?"

"Don't look now, but it looks like you're going to spend the next five courses bumping elbows with him!"

Meg's eyes went wide, and she spun around. "Oh, my God," she breathed to Kate. "What am I going to say to him?"

"Relax, Meg. Everybody understands that you lefties have a hard time at the dinner table," Kate said, not managing to suppress a smile.

"Kate, he's looking at me!"

"Remember what your teacher taught you in kindergarten? Just be yourself and everyone will like you."

Meg took a deep breath and walked to her chair

with as much poise as she could muster. Tim stood next to his seat, and Meg thought it looked as if he was waiting for her. *You're dreaming,* she said to herself. *Even Gretchen thinks this guy is out of your league . . . but boy, does he look good!* Surreptitiously rubbing her damp palms against the sides of her dress, she resolved to play it cool and act as though she'd never seen him before.

Tim turned to Meg, his eyes glued to hers. "Hi, I'm Tim Wilson," he said. "I think we're dinner partners."

Meg felt her pulse accelerate to what felt like a hundred beats a second. *This is your chance, Meg. Don't blow it.* "Uh, nice to meet you. I'm Megan Henry." *Oh, great line,* Meg thought. *Just what Annette Bening probably said to Warren Beatty.*

"Well, Megan, I'm guessing they put us together because we're the only ones here under twenty-five and over six. It must be fate." Tim grinned and stared at Meg with an intensity that took her breath away.

"Caroline's my cousin. I was a bridesmaid," Meg blurted out as they sat down.

"Yeah, I noticed. Uh, you did a good job of walking down the aisle. I've seen a lot of bridesmaids bolt down to the altar like they were running a fifty-meter sprint."

"Luckily I've been walking for quite some time now. It took a lot of practice, but I finally got it right."

"Congratulations," Tim said, laughing.

"So, Tim." Meg tried to sound nonchalant. "How do you know Rick and Caroline, anyway?"

"Rick's my soccer coach."

Awesome, Meg thought. *He doesn't realize that I know who he is. Maybe I really can create a whole new me tonight.* She'd pretend that talking with Tim was no big deal. Maybe she could even convince herself of that! "Oh, yeah," she said aloud. "Now that you remind me, I think I saw you in a couple of games." *A couple of thousand, that is.*

Across the table, Kate and Gloria grinned at Meg. Kate flashed her a discreet thumbs-up sign, and Gloria tipped an imaginary hat. Two of Rick's groomsmen, Frankie and David, were arguing about fraternity hazing, oblivious to the rest of them.

Meg racked her brain for something witty to say to Tim. She noticed unhappily that he seemed content to eat his salad and stare from time to time at the ceiling of the tent. *He's probably trying to think of a way to escape. He's probably wondering if anyone would believe that he got a quick but severe case of food poisoning from the Boston lettuce.*

Finally Tim turned to Meg and cleared his throat. "So, Megan, what do you think of hazing?"

"Well, from what I hear, fraternities and sororities sound pretty messed up. I don't like the idea of being judged by a bunch of snobby girls."

"You've got that right. I mean, forget hazing. No one's making me wear women's clothes at noon in the quad! And I'm definitely not up for having a couple of sweaty football players hold me upside down by the ankles while I drink from a keg tap and everyone yells, 'Chug! Chug! Chug!'"

Meg laughed at the image. "Yeah, I think you're better on your feet."

"So you didn't rush when you got here last semester?" Tim asked.

"Oh, I don't go to the university," Meg stammered.

"You're one of those Vermillion College girls, huh?"

Meg's brain whirled. He actually thought she was a freshman at the women's college. What would he say when he found out that she didn't even have her driver's license? Meg stalled for time as the waiters brought around the Dijon chicken that was being served for dinner. At last she made a vague sound that was somewhere between yes and no. "Vermillion doesn't have sororities," she said clearly.

"College is great, don't you think?" Tim asked. "No more rules, no more parents telling you what to do. I wouldn't go back to high school if you put a gun to my head!"

This is it, Meg thought. *If I tell him the truth, he'll be gone before dessert. But if I lie . . . What's the worst that can happen?* "High school? Those are two words I never want to hear in the same sentence again!"

Meg had thought that Kate and Gloria were engrossed in a teasing match with Frankie and David. But when she glanced away from Tim, she saw that they were looking at her with raised eyebrows. "Really, Meg," Gloria called. "To think we knew you when you were a lowly tenth grader. I can remember it like it was just this morning!"

"Want to take a little walk before dessert is served?" Tim pushed back his chair and stood up.

"Good idea. We can check out what the rest of the block is doing tonight." Meg put her napkin on the table and waved at Gloria. "We'll be right back," she told them.

"Have fun, kids," Kate said. "But come back in time for cake and ice cream!"

Meg grimaced.

Tim shook his head and laughed. "You seniors can't keep up with the young'uns. Come on, Meg."

As Meg followed Tim from the table he casually grabbed her hand. Her heart thumped, and she looked around to make sure her parents were nowhere in sight. They probably wouldn't appreciate the sight of their daughter walking off into the night hand in hand with a college guy.

When they reached the front yard, Tim guided Meg down the path to the quiet street. "So, Meg. Tell me everything."

"Such as?" Did everything include her real age?

"For starters, what are you going to major in?"

That was an easy one. "English," she answered.

"What's your focus?" He kicked a rock down the street. "Sorry. Kicking round objects in my path is a habit."

"Focus?"

"You know. Medieval literature? The modern novel? Romantic poetry?"

"Oh, right, my focus. Um, modern novels, I think. I have a special fondness for the modern anti-hero." She smiled to herself. Not bad for a high school girl.

"Anti-heroes, huh?" Tim laughed. "I'll have to remember that in the future."

"What about you?" She tried to guess at his major. Business? History?

"Political science. I'm trying to get an internship in D.C. this summer . . . at least, I was."

"You're not now?" They reached the end of the block and turned back toward Caroline's. Meg could hear the band tuning their instruments. "How come?"

Tim shrugged. "It's a long story. Anyway, I still might go. Let's just say I have some reservations."

"Sounds interesting. Care to elaborate?"

"Not really. Summer's still a long way off. Let's talk about tonight. I feel like we're existing outside of time. Almost like we're on a different planet."

Meg nodded. She'd been thinking the same thing for the last few hours.

"So, tell me something real about you. Not your major, or your favorite color. Tell me something that's going to make me know you."

"Okay. Ask me a question, and I'll answer it."

Tim thought for a moment. "What do you value more than anything else? And I don't mean making the dean's list, or getting into a good seminar."

Meg didn't have to think before she responded. "Freedom. Real freedom. I crave it. And love, I guess. The combination of those two things would be dizzying."

Tim nodded. "But sometimes I wonder if they're mutually exclusive. If you give freedom to someone you love, they might run away."

"Then it's not real love," Meg answered. "And you're better off alone."

Tim squeezed her hand. "You're right, Meg. I've been needing to hear someone say just that." He stopped walking and turned to face her. "I'm glad that someone was you."

"Me too." For a second she forgot that Tim was older, more experienced. She even forgot that they barely knew each other. Talking to him, she felt as though they were picking up an ongoing conversation—not just getting to know each other. They took a few steps in silence. "Your turn. What do you value the most?" Meg asked.

"Hmm . . . I'll have to ponder that for a second."

Meg watched Tim's face as he thought. She needed to tell him the truth about her age. With him believing she was in college, none of this experience was real. She took a deep breath. "Tim—"

"Honesty," he said suddenly. "Any kind of deception makes me crazy. If someone's honest from the get-go, you know you can depend on them. But if they lie, or deliberately keep something from you, then there's no hope. The trust is gone."

His voice was grim and bitter. Meg knew it was definitely not the time to reveal her age. If the night was going to continue to be magical, she'd have to keep her secret to herself.

As they neared the lawn Meg could see her mom walking among the tables. Was she searching for her? She quickly let go of Tim's hand. "I'm going to run ahead. I see my mom, and I, uh, need to ask her where she put something of mine earlier."

Tim raised his eyebrows. "Okay. I'll meet you in front of our dessert plates."

"It's a date."

Tim held Meg close as they danced. The wedding band, Heaven Sent, was playing their own version of "It Had to Be You." *Heaven Sent is right*, Meg thought dreamily. *This last hour has been divine!*

Meg could feel each of Tim's five long fingers pressing firmly against the small of her back. The delicious searing sensation his warm hand generated through the thin material of her dress sent sparks shooting all the way up her spine. Even the slightly rough, masculine texture of his tux jacket made the tips of her fingers tingle.

The last of the cherries jubilee had been cleared away and toasts had been made. Strings of white lights twinkled everywhere, and the fragrance of dozens of roses filled the air. When the members of the six-piece band had played their first song Meg felt a thrill of anticipation. *Thank goodness Mom and Dad are sitting at the other end of the tent for dinner,* she'd said to herself. *I would die if Dad came up to the table and called me Sweet Potato!*

Now that she was dancing with Tim, Meg felt as if she were starring in one of those black-and-white movies from the forties. Better yet, it was as if she really had stepped into the fairy tale she'd been dreaming about earlier. She was dancing the night away in glass slippers, a handsome prince holding her tight. *Will I turn into a pumpkin at midnight?* Meg wondered as Tim gently tucked a loose strand of hair behind her ear.

Their conversation during dessert had been good but nerve-racking. She'd held her breath a couple of times when she'd thought someone was about to blow her cover. And she'd had to do some lightning-quick thinking when Tim asked her which of the college libraries she usually studied in. She'd almost slipped up and said that she could get most of her homework done during study hall.

I couldn't keep this act up for long. It's exhausting, Meg thought, inching closer to Tim. Thank goodness he'd stopped his string of questions.

In fact, since the music started, Meg hadn't needed to speak at all. She and Tim had drifted to the dance floor, joining the other couples who were swaying to the romantic music. Meg saw Rick and Caroline nearby, and she caught her cousin's eye. Caroline winked at Meg as Rick dipped her extravagantly.

"I could tango all night," Meg challenged Tim.

"So could I," Meg heard a voice behind her respond.

"Dad! I didn't see you there," Meg squeaked.

"Mind if I cut in?" Mr. Henry looked pointedly at Tim.

Meg was too happy to feel embarrassed. Tim squeezed her hand and stepped aside. "I'll be watching you," he whispered in her ear.

Caroline stood at the top of the front steps of the house. Below her, Meg and the other unmarried girls gathered to wait for Caroline to throw her bouquet. *I wonder if Gretchen's premonition will come true,* Meg thought, picturing herself showing off a diamond engagement ring in the high school cafeteria. *Maybe Tim is the guy I'm meant to be with forever. . . .*

Laurie, one of the other bridesmaids, put an arm around Meg's shoulders. "I guess our power makeover did the trick—Tim Wilson can't keep his eyes off you!" she said in a stage whisper.

"Is he really looking over here?" Meg resisted

the urge to crane her neck and search out Tim.
"Laurie, isn't he the most gorgeous, intelligent guy
you've ever met? I think I'm in love!"

"Whoa, girl. Slow down! Tim seems like a great
guy—but he's nineteen years old! In other words,
it's fine if he looks, but he'd better not touch."

Meg could feel her frustration rising. The past
few hours had been perfect. Now Laurie insisted
on reminding Meg of that dull, immature identity
she thought she'd shed at Caroline's dressing table.
"Mmm," Meg answered noncommittally.

"Heads up!" Caroline suddenly yelled. Meg stood
on her tiptoes and thrust her hands up high. She
saw the flowers sailing through the air, and for a
moment she thought they would fly over her head.
And then Meg felt the bouquet hit her hands; she
clutched it tightly, bringing it down close to her chest.
Everyone erupted into cheers, and she heard several
people call out her name. Meg blushed and held her
prize up for everyone to see. *I can't wait to tell
Gretchen,* she thought. *She's going to hyperventilate!*

Lined up on either side of the front walk, guests
stood holding small baskets filled with pink, purple,
and white tissue-paper hearts. Quickly Meg and the
other girls retrieved baskets and joined the rest of
the group. At a signal from her mother, Caroline
and Rick ran hand in hand down the front steps.
Instead of rice, the guests threw handfuls of the tissue hearts at the bride and groom, calling out good
wishes and laughing.

The luminaria-dotted lawn provided enough
light so that the brightly colored tissue paper stood
out against the dark sky. Meg watched the whirl of

hearts fluttering softly to the ground and waved as Rick and Caroline hopped into the red convertible Mustang that waited at the curb. Their driver was Frankie, the groomsman who'd been sitting at Meg's table; he peeled away from the curb honking and sped down the street, a trail of tin cans bouncing and clattering behind.

"Meg, tonight has been really great. I think this day will be imprinted on my brain forever," Tim said softly.

They stood at the edge of the lawn, away from the lights and noise of the party. Meg could feel the pulse at her throat beating rapidly. *He's going to kiss me. I can't believe this is happening.* "Tim, you're . . . you're . . . well, I've had an amazing time, too!"

In one hand, Meg still held Caroline's wedding bouquet. Tim reached for her other hand and pulled her close to him. He ran his fingers over the soft skin of her cheek and tucked a loose tendril of hair behind her ear. Meg sucked in her breath. *Please don't let me make an idiot of myself,* she prayed silently.

Tim traced her lips with his thumb as Meg stared into his eyes, mesmerized. "You're very beautiful, Megan Henry," he whispered. Slowly Tim bent his head until his lips were just inches from hers.

"Do I seem like one of your modern anti-heroes?" he asked quietly. "Am I dangerous, confused, angst-ridden?" His soft voice sent shivers up her spine.

She shook her head slowly. "You may be more dangerous than you realize," she whispered.

"Let's hope so, for both our sakes."

Then he kissed her. His lips were warm and gentle, and Meg could feel her body's instant response. She put her arms around his neck as he pulled her closer. For a moment she opened her eyes and looked up at the dark night. The moon seemed so close that she wanted to reach out and grab it. Then she shut her eyes, savoring the silky feel of Tim's hair against her fingers.

When they broke apart a minute later, Meg was flushed with happiness. Earlier Tim had been barely more than a figment of her imagination. Although she'd felt the warmth of his body as they danced, he hadn't seemed real. He was a being she'd conjured up—the dream guy who was going to complete her night of fantasy with a kiss on the hand and a quick bow. After she'd caught the bouquet, Meg had half expected to see the silhouette of Tim's back retreating down the block, possibly disintegrating before her very eyes.

But the touch of his lips against hers made him real. A phantom kiss couldn't have turned her insides into liquid. Meg brushed her lips with two of her fingers. She'd been kissed several times before, but now she saw that none of the others had really counted. *Yes*, Meg thought, *this was my first real kiss, and it was wonderful. Gretchen's going to faint when she finds out!*

"Wasn't it a beautiful wedding, Meg?" her mother asked as she turned around to smile at Meg in the back seat.

Meg had been gazing out the car window, her

mind packed full of images of Tim. She'd given him her phone number, and she was already counting the minutes until he called. If he called. And that was a big if. "What?" she asked her mother blankly. "I mean, yes, it was beautiful."

"Who was that boy you were talking with for so long?"

"Oh, just some guy. He plays on Rick's soccer team," Meg answered, trying to sound casual. *Just some guy who's probably the best thing that ever happened to me . . .*

Three

At the sound of the doorbell, Meg switched off her stereo and raced down the stairs. The lyrics of Billie Holiday's "Let's Fall in Love" echoed in her mind as she danced the last few steps down the hallway. She swung the front door open and executed an almost perfect pirouette.

"Excuse me, I thought I was at the Henrys' house. This seems to be a rehearsal for the Miss America pageant." Gretchen stood on the doorstep, an old Kermit the Frog towel hanging off one shoulder. Sunlight glinted off her dark hair, and her brown eyes squinted up at Meg.

"Very funny, Fetchin' Gretchen," Meg said. "Has Southwest High School imposed a new law against enthusiasm that I should know about?"

Gretchen walked into the Henrys' foyer and looked pointedly at the pink high heels that completed

Meg's outfit of denim cut-offs and an old I Love New York T-shirt.

"I have two theories—no, make that three. One: You danced so much last night that your feet swelled irrevocably and those heels are now permanently attached to your body."

"Wrong."

"Two: You've decided to blow off high school and try to make it as a runway model."

"Guess again. This is getting interesting." Meg shut the front door and led Gretchen toward the kitchen.

"Three: You know how much I hate being short, and you're mocking me for some sadistic reason that I can't even guess at without collecting further data." Gretchen put her hands on her hips and waited.

Meg kicked off her heels, one of which landed in the sink full of dirty dishes with a loud clatter. "Four: Last night was the best night of my life, and these shoes are a little reminder of it. I'd wear the dress, but I don't think it's meant for sunbathing in the backyard."

Gretchen laughed. "Now *that's* what I call interesting. You'd better not be planning on keeping me in suspense."

"Don't worry, Gretch. I'm ready to spill some major guts."

Meg grabbed a six-pack of diet soda from the refrigerator. Then she reached under the sink for her special spray bottle of coconut-scented tanning oil. Armed and ready to sweat, the girls went out to the two battered lounge chairs in Meg's backyard.

Gretchen stripped off her sundress and revealed a red tank suit that had been around since junior high swim team. She settled back against Kermit's smiling face and propped a pair of electric-blue heart-shaped sunglasses on her nose. "Okay, let's make sure we're on the same wavelength here," she said, glancing over to the other chair, where Meg was spraying herself with suntan oil. "During the last episode of *Meg: Young and Frustrated,* our heroine, the beautiful but misguided Megan Henry, was hoping to be swept off her feet by a tall, dark, and handsome college man. If I remember correctly, the show ended with a cliffhanger—"

"That was a daytime soap opera," Meg interrupted. "Let me tell you about the prime-time miniseries."

"Was there nudity?" Gretchen asked hopefully.

"Please! Gretchen, this is serious." Meg sighed and let her thoughts drift back to the night before, to the dark edge of the lawn, where Tim had taken her in his arms. How could she explain to Gretchen the perfect crescent of moon that had been shining above Tim's head? How could she describe the way she'd been shaking all over, even though her hands had been steady as she ran her fingers through Tim's hair?

Megan wanted to shout and sing; she wanted to dance out every detail of the previous night. Instead she felt as though every word out of her mouth was cotton candy—sweet, but insignificant.

Gretchen turned to Meg, her eyebrows raised in a question. "Was it Tim Wilson? Did you get to dance with him?"

"Oh, we danced." Meg stopped for a dramatic pause. "And he kissed me—for a long time."

"I don't believe it!" Gretchen squealed. "I mean, I believe it, but it's hard to believe. A college guy kissed you!"

"He's not just a college guy. He happens to be the most wonderful man on earth. I think I'm in love. Scratch that—I know I'm in love!" Meg beamed at Gretchen.

"This is so incredibly romantic. Who would have thought that Tim Wilson would fall for a lowly fifteen-year-old? I guess it's true that the heart knows no age."

"There is one minor detail that I should probably mention," Meg said, pulling at the leg opening of her yellow bikini and checking the progress of her tan line.

"What? He's a Soviet spy? He's really a woman? He—"

"He thinks I'm a freshman in college," Meg cut in, suddenly absorbed in the contrast of her skin tones.

Gretchen let out a low whistle. She sat forward abruptly, and Kermit the Frog's face crumpled as the towel slid down the back of her chair.

"And why, may I ask, does he think you're in college?"

"I think it has something to do with the fact that I told him I live in Carman Hall. Or it might be the way I was complaining about Professor Gately's Buddhist Theories class." Meg thanked heaven she had paid close attention as Caroline's college career unfolded—and had a good enough imagination to fill in the differences between Caroline's experiences at the university and her own fictional account of life at Vermillion.

"Meg, this is not a minor detail. A paper cut or a tiny zit on your chin is minor. This is major—this is a huge whopper of a lie."

"I know, I know. But what was I supposed to do? He *assumed* I was in college. It didn't seem like a big deal to let him believe it. The whole night was just so . . . unreal." Meg paused, searching for words that would make Gretchen understand her rash lie. There were none. "Anyway, I feel like I *should* be in college. You know how sick I am of algebra and pep club bake sales."

"Yeah, yeah. Freedom and the open road, right? Meg, how many times do I have to remind you that you don't even have your driver's license? For you, the open road is the seven blocks of sidewalk that lead from your house to mine."

"Another minor detail?" Meg questioned. She hated the way Gretchen could make her feel like a guilty child.

"I think you need to grow up and be young and immature like the rest of us."

"Gretch, don't you understand? I just want to enjoy this. I really think I'm in love with Tim. Don't spoil it with a lecture—I need a best friend, not another mother."

"Okay, I give in. I'm happy for you."

"Thank you!"

"Just one more question. What if your parents find out?"

Meg winced. "Can we talk about something

pleasant? Like the threat of nuclear war or the destruction of the ozone layer?"

"Don't mind me," Gretchen responded. "I'm just a voice of reason. Think of me as yin to your yang."

"How was Michael Levy's barbecue?" Meg decided to cut her losses and move on to a safer topic of conversation.

"It was so great," Gretchen began enthusiastically. "There were lots of juniors there. Even a few seniors. Grant Janes brought his guitar, and we had a short but eventful whipped-cream fight—luckily there were only a couple of cans of the stuff floating around."

"Sounds like fun," Meg said politely.

She couldn't believe how different her Saturday night had been from her best friend's. While Meg had been talking to Tim about foreign films and Virginia Woolf's books, Gretchen had been singing old camp tunes. And Meg couldn't imagine a whipped-cream fight qualifying as "great." Only a week before, she would have been thrilled to be around high-school seniors. Now Meg felt that there was a whole world outside high school that she might actually get to be a part of.

"I haven't told you the best thing." Gretchen grinned.

"What?"

"Billy Jenkins asked about you."

"He did? What did he say?"

"He said, 'Where's Meg?' and I said, 'She's at her cousin's wedding.' Then—get this—he said, 'Too bad. I thought she was going to be here.' Is that awesome or what?"

"Wow, he sure has a way with words. Maybe we could get that engraved on a gold plaque."

"Well, excuse me. I forgot that you were in *college*. Of course the words of a mere junior in high school would be boring to a sophisticated coed."

"I didn't mean it like that, and you know it."

"I know. I just hope you're not getting in over your head, Meg. I'd hate to see you washed up and heartbroken before we've even gone to the junior prom." Gretchen closed her eyes and tilted her face toward the sun. The conversation was over.

Meg stared at the U.S. history book in her lap. She thought about the lives of sophomores in high school a hundred years from the present. Would they be bogged down with an extra thousand pages of textbook to cover the years between now and then—or would teachers exclude a few decades from the curriculum? Maybe in the twenty-first century kids wouldn't have to know who the first mayor of Jamestown was, or how much the Dutch paid the Native Americans for New York. Maybe history class would start with an in-depth study of fashions during the disco era. . . .

Meg's book landed next to her nightstand with a thud. Who was she kidding? The only thought her brain could fully form was that she wished Tim Wilson would call. *If he doesn't call tonight, I'll forget about him. I might lie down and die, but I'll forget about him.*

It was Monday night. She'd known he wouldn't call Sunday night—no self-respecting guy would call a girl the very next day after he kissed her. He had to wait a night, not appear too eager. Meg figured that rule never changed. But he had to call that night. It was essential.

Meg looked at the phone expectantly. Thank goodness her parents had gotten fed up with her endless hours of tying up the phone and given her a separate line when she was thirteen. She would have died of humiliation if Tim called and her mother—even worse, her *father*—answered! But she was getting ahead of herself. So far the phone hadn't rung at all.

Meg was so intent on watching the phone that when it actually rang she jumped, startled by the sharp sound in her silent room.

On the third ring, she answered. "Hello?"

"Did he call?" Gretchen's voice was eager.

"Oh, it's you."

"I'll take that as a no," Gretchen answered. The sympathy in her voice brought a lump to Meg's throat.

"It's not even nine o'clock. He could still be at the library." Meg forced her voice to sound casual.

"He's probably playing it cool. Unless—"

"Unless what?"

"Well, there's always the chance that he found out the truth."

"Don't even think it. Listen, I'll call you later. I have a lot of homework."

"In other words, you don't want Tim to get a busy signal while you're wasting your time talking to me."

"Precisely." Meg wondered why she even bothered

trying to slip lies past Gretchen. The girl was a walking polygraph test.

"Bye."

Meg hung up the phone and lay down on her side, tucking her knees up beneath her chin. *I will not cry, I will not cry.* She repeated the words to herself over and over.

With a sick feeling in her stomach, she forced herself to consider the night of the wedding again. What had happened, really? Some conversation, a few dances, one perfect kiss . . . Lots of people had danced. And lots of people had kissed. It would have been impossible for the love between Rick and Caroline not to have rubbed off on everyone else. Maybe Tim had even meant all the things he'd said right before he kissed her. But those emotions were frozen in time; once the romance of the evening was over and Tim had gotten back to his dorm room, he'd probably laughed at himself for getting so caught up in the moment.

Meg sighed. It was time that she laughed at herself, too. Being with Tim had been wonderful—out-of-this-world wonderful. But if she didn't let her feeling dissolve the way an exquisitely sculptured ice statue melts in the sun, then she'd be caught in a trap of unrequited longing until the end of time.

The phone rang again, and Meg shook her head. Why couldn't Gretchen let her be miserable in peace? She groaned and reached for the receiver on the first ring.

"What now?" she asked wearily.

"Are you always this friendly, or are you in training to be the world's worst receptionist?"

At the sound of Tim's husky voice, Meg's heart plunged to her feet.

"Tim! I'm sorry, I thought you were someone else." Meg's voice sounded high and unnatural to her ears.

"No problem. Just remind me not to call when you're in a bad mood."

"Can we start this conversation over?"

Meg heard Tim's soft laughter on the other end of the line. Her heart slowed down to somewhere near its normal rate, and she lounged against the fluffy white pillows that were piled against the headboard of her bed.

"Of course. First I'll say, 'Hi, Meg, this is Tim.' Now, since my insecurities come spewing forth when I call a beautiful woman, I'll add a really dumb-sounding sentence clarifying my identity: 'I'm the guy you sat next to during Caroline and Rick's wedding reception.'"

"Tim! I think I remember. Weren't you the one who spilled cherry sauce on his cummerbund?" Meg turned on her bed for a view of the bouquet she'd caught at the wedding. Her mother had hung the flowers upside down on the wall above her desk, so that the petals would maintain their shape as they dried. Meg had started to think of the bouquet as the centerpiece of her room.

Again the sound of his laughter made the blood rush to her head. Meg wished she could tape-record the moment and play it over and over again once it had passed.

"How've you been?"

"Good," Meg answered. "I've . . . I've been thinking about you." Meg wanted to punch herself.

How could she have said something so totally corny? *Tim is probably gagging. He's probably looking over at his roommate and pretending to stick his finger down his throat.*

"Megan, you don't know how glad I am to hear you say that. I've been worrying about calling you for the last twenty-four hours. I kept wondering, 'Will she think I'm a loser if I call her now?' Then five minutes later I'd say to myself, 'How about now?'"

"Will you do me a favor?"

"Anything."

"When in doubt, *call me!*"

As they continued talking Meg's lies faded from her mind. She could talk to Tim in a way that the boys she'd dated before would have laughed at. And there were no awkward pauses in their conversation. Meg didn't have to pretend to hear her mother's voice calling her so she'd have an excuse to get off the phone.

When she finally set the phone gently in its cradle it was past eleven o'clock. The idea of calling Gretchen flitted through Meg's mind. But she wasn't in the mood for Gretchen's probing or well-meaning reprimands. She just wanted to savor the past hour, turning Tim's words over and over in her head.

When she finally turned her light out, the last thing Tim had said reverberated in Meg's ears like the sound of church bells ringing on a quiet Sunday morning. "I'll see you Saturday," he had said.

I'll see you Saturday. Meg thought those four words were more poetic than any of the Shakespearean sonnets she'd read in Mr. Quigly's English class the previous semester. If she could only get through the week ahead, Meg would see Tim on Saturday. Nothing short of malaria would keep her from making that date.

The same moon that she'd seen over Tim's head on Saturday was shining through her window. Just before she shut her eyes, Meg gazed at the moon. "I'll see you Saturday," she whispered.

Four

    The lunch line seemed particularly long on Tuesday. As Meg waited for her turn to choose between a bowl of green Jell-O and a butterscotch brownie, she scanned the cafeteria for Gretchen. Meg and Gretchen had eaten lunch together every day since the beginning of their freshman year, and Meg considered the half hour sacred.

    She spotted Gretchen sitting with two of their friends, Jane Sullivan and Maria Sanchez, at a table near the far window. Meg smiled with anticipation at the thought of the dramatic announcement she would make in a few moments. She couldn't wait to see the expression on the other girls' faces when they found out that Tim Wilson had asked her on a real date.

    Holding her tray up at shoulder level, Meg made her way through the noisy cafeteria. Gretchen's voice rose above the din of clattering silverware, and Meg called out to her. When the three girls caught sight of Meg, they stopped talking and looked down at their plates of turkey tetrazzini.

Meg slid into the seat between Gretchen and Maria and cast a puzzled glance at her friends. "What's up with all of you? Do I have mashed potatoes in my hair or something?"

"No, no," Gretchen answered, patting Meg's shoulder. "We were just saying that if a certain guy didn't call a certain girl last night, it doesn't really mean anything. He might have had homework, or been watching a basketball game on TV or something."

"So you were talking about me."

Jane chewed on her bottom lip. "Meg, we were just speaking hypothetically. Like, say the girl wrote her phone number down on a napkin—the guy could have lost it."

"Yeah," Maria interrupted. "That happens all the time in the movies. Sometimes ill-fated lovers are kept apart for a lifetime, just because the dumb guy accidentally left the girl's number in a cab."

Meg made a show of clearing her throat, and three pairs of eyes turned to stare at her. "If you all aren't too engrossed in this *hypothetical* conversation—and I must admit, it *is* fascinating—I have something to tell you!"

"What?" Gretchen asked.

"Tim called!" Meg grinned triumphantly and surveyed the expressions on her friends' faces.

"He did? When?" Gretchen gasped.

"Wow!" Jane interjected.

"Tell us *everything*," Maria said, turning her chair so that she was only inches from Meg.

"I don't really know what to say. He called, and we talked, and it was great!"

"And?" Jane prompted.

"And we're going out on Saturday," Meg said simply, waiting for the news to sink into her friends' minds.

"Do you think you can handle it?" Maria questioned.

"What do you mean?"

"Being in college sounds a lot different from being in high school. Are you sure you can pull it off?"

Meg was surprised by Maria's probing. Meg had told Jane and Maria about her night with Tim, but she'd conveniently left out the fact that she'd lied to him about her age. *Gretchen must have told them behind my back,* Meg realized.

"You're going to be up to your earrings in lies before the end of the date!" Jane added unnecessarily.

"Wait a second," Meg exclaimed. "A minute ago you guys were spilling over with hypothetical reasons why Tim wouldn't have called. Now that you know he has, you're treating me like I'm in the KGB."

"Sorry, Meg," Maria said with a sheepish smile. "I really am happy for you. I just don't know if I'd have the guts to go out with a guy who thought I was in college."

Jane nodded in agreement with Maria.

"It's not like that," Meg said, shrugging. "When I'm with him, age seems totally unimportant. I'll tell him the truth—eventually."

Gretchen had been sitting quietly until that

moment. "Why didn't you tell me he called?" she burst out suddenly, her voice high and shrill.

Meg was taken aback by Gretchen's angry tone. She'd expected a shout of victory, maybe a hug. But Gretchen's face had turned stony, and she was glaring at Meg.

"I'm telling you now," Meg said.

"Obviously you're telling me now," Gretchen snapped. "I just don't understand why you didn't call me last night. You *knew* I was waiting to hear from you."

"It was late when I got off the phone with Tim— I didn't want to bother you."

Jane and Maria sat in silence, turning their heads in unison to look first at Gretchen, then at Meg.

"Meg, Tim Wilson is the biggest thing that's happened to you since Nelson Eubanks kissed you during spin the bottle in fourth grade. How could you think one measly phone call was going to *bother* me?" Gretchen was shouting.

"Jeez, Gretch, calm down. To be honest, I just didn't feel like talking to anyone last night. I wanted to think about Tim without any of these stupid worries about my age ruining everything."

"Excuse me for worrying about my best friend," Gretchen said, her voice sullen.

"Anyway," Meg continued, "it looks like I was right not to have said anything before. None of you is exactly brimming over with good wishes. To think I expected you to be excited for me!"

"We are excited," Jane said.

"We just don't want to see you get hurt," Maria added.

Meg stood up, the tray with her half-eaten lunch in her hands. "I am *not* going to get hurt. In fact, right now all I can think about is how sorry I am that my friends are stuck mooning over guys who don't even have their licenses yet!"

Meg stalked away with her head high. She forced her steps to be steady, but inside she was trembling. *Am I crazy?* she wondered. *If my best friends don't think this relationship stands a chance, then how am I going to convince myself that it does?*

Saturday morning, Meg stepped off the bus at Fourteenth Street and Delaware Avenue. Walking the last couple of blocks to Moody's Diner, where she'd arranged to meet Tim at ten o'clock, Meg tried to squeeze out of her mind the doubts that had been nagging at her for the last few days. *What if Tim doesn't even recognize me?* she thought. *Or what if I walk into the diner and he's sitting in a back booth with another girl?*

Meg could picture Tim sipping black coffee with a college cheerleader. Maybe when he saw Meg he would wave casually and turn with a smile to the cheerleader. "Jeannie," he would say (Meg was sure the girl's name would be one of those cutesy -*ie* names she couldn't stand), "this is Caroline's little cousin, the one I was telling you about. She wants to get a taste of what the big kids do for fun."

Meg saw Tim the second she walked into Moody's. In worn khakis and an olive-green oxford shirt, he took her breath away, just as he had in his tux the Saturday before. When he looked in her eyes and smiled, Meg felt her fears melt away.

Questions whirling in her head, Meg stood transfixed while Tim walked toward her. *Will he kiss me, right here in the middle of the restaurant? Should I shake his hand? And if he reaches for my hand, should I give him a firm, businesslike handshake— or should I let my hand rest in his softly, the way a woman in a French movie would?*

Meg's questions receded into the background when Tim enveloped her in a warm hug.

"It's been a long week," he greeted her.

"We're here now," Meg returned.

As they slid into a secluded booth Meg took in the college-soaked atmosphere of Moody's. She loved the tattered posters that covered the walls, advertising everything from folk music festivals to a Young Republicans rally. Scanning the predictable diner menu, Meg allowed herself to forget—at least temporarily—that she wasn't really a college student. With Tim across the table from her it was easy to believe that she went there every weekend. Meg could even imagine herself in Moody's at dawn, falling asleep over a cup of bad coffee after a grueling all-nighter during finals.

"I have a confession to make." Tim's voice broke the awkward silence that had been between them since they sat down.

So do I, Meg said to herself. "What is it?" she asked aloud.

"I got here an hour early, just to make sure we got a good booth."

Meg loved the way Tim's eyes crinkled when he

smiled at her. She must have imagined those eyes
a million times during the last week.

"I have a confession to make, too."

"Let me guess. Option A: You woke up this
morning and contemplated blowing off our date.
Option B: You've been walking around the block
for an hour feeling almost as nervous as I have."
Tim leaned back and waited for Meg's answer.

"Option B is close. Actually, I've been up since
seven, feeling nervous in my room." Meg laughed,
but a knot formed in her stomach. What if he knew
her real confession?

What would Tim think if he knew that she'd gotten up at seven to make sure she'd have time to
recreate the girl he'd met the other night? She'd
stood in her bathroom, a counter full of blush, lip
liners, and eye makeup in front of her. Half an
hour with her blow dryer had helped her achieve a
smooth, middle-part hairstyle that she'd seen on
girls around the university campus. Assembling the
perfect outfit had taken another agonizing forty-five
minutes. She'd started the morning in a floral calf-
length sundress. But by the time she'd walked out
the front door, shouting a hasty, garbled good-bye
to her parents, Meg was dressed in a pair of faded
men's Levi's from the secondhand store and a
tight-fitting black bodysuit. Her thick-soled
espadrilles added at least an inch to her height, and
she hoped the jangling silver jewelry she'd chosen
gave her an artistic flair.

Tim set his menu on the table and pulled his
long fingers through his carefully combed hair. "I'm
glad I wasn't the only one feeling nervous," he

said. "Now that we've established that we were both a little nervous this morning, let's put the butterflies behind us. Deal?"

"Deal," Meg answered, although she could still feel about a million butterflies taking flight in the pit of her stomach.

"Let's shake on it," Tim said, reaching across the table to clasp Meg's hand in a firm grip.

The tingle Meg felt from just the touch of Tim's hand caught her by surprise; she was glad when the waitress appeared to take their orders.

As the waitress made her way back toward the kitchen of the noisy diner, Tim turned a steady gaze on Meg.

"So what's the quickest, most direct route into Megan Henry's heart?"

"Ah, cruise down Stratford Road and then take a left on Sunset Drive?" Meg quipped, giving Tim directions to the dorm where she'd told him she lived.

"Seriously."

"Seriously . . ." Meg paused, wanting to give Tim a real answer. Wanting to ask him the same question. "I don't know. I guess I've never met anyone who's found a way—direct or otherwise—into my heart."

"And now?"

"I think it's a distinct possibility."

Eleven hours later, Tim stopped his blue Oldsmobile convertible in front of Carman Hall. Before Meg had a chance to unfasten her seat belt, Tim reached out and placed a warm hand on the back of her neck. With his other hand, he held Meg's chin firmly in place. She couldn't have turned her gaze away from his midnight-blue eyes even if she'd wanted to.

Meg's heart came to an alarming halt inside her chest as she waited for Tim to kiss her. But instead of touching her lips with his, Tim leaned forward and rubbed his forehead against Meg's.

"You know, you're a great roller coaster partner." He smiled. "I think those fingernail marks you put in my arm are permanent—sort of a free tattoo."

"I warned you about me and heights," Meg returned defensively. "You have to admit, though, my ear-splitting screams did make Thunder Mountain pretty exciting!"

After breakfast, Tim had driven Megan to a small amusement park on the outskirts of town. They'd stayed all day, finally watching the sunset from the Ferris wheel. As they'd driven away from the park Meg had turned around in the car to watch the lights of the rides recede into the dark night. *Wherever Tim and I are*, she had thought, *bright lights twinkle over our heads.*

Tim's eyes held an amused glimmer as he regarded Meg. "Yeah, the people in line at Thunder Mountain thought your screaming was so exciting that they all bailed on the roller coaster and made a beeline for the bumper cars."

"You can laugh now, Tim Wilson. But I remember hearing a few shrieks from the seat next to mine!"

"Those were just for show—I wanted an excuse to put my arm around you," Tim responded. Then he drew Meg toward him and fixed her full lips with a heavy stare.

Involuntarily Meg ran her tongue over her dry lips. Before she finished, Tim closed the last inch between them, covering her mouth with his. As the feel of Tim's soft, warm lips sank into Meg's consciousness, she experienced a curious melting sensation. She tried to form rational thoughts about the sensations that coursed through her, but her mind was totally devoted to the need to return Tim's kiss.

After Tim drew away, Meg realized that she was still sitting slightly forward, her chin tilted up, as if she were posing for one of Robert Doisneau's kiss posters. When Meg turned to study Tim's profile, she saw a small vein pulsing in his temple. *Is that because of me?* she wondered, a slow red blush creeping up her neck and over her cheeks.

"Which room is yours?" Tim asked suddenly, nodding his head in the direction of Carman Hall.

Meg's eyes darted up and down the ivy-covered dorm. Fervently wishing that she didn't have to tell such bald-faced lies, Meg picked out a room on one of the upper floors. Its light was turned off and the shade was drawn.

"It's that one," she said, pointing.

As Tim's glance followed the line of Meg's finger to the dark window, the room was suddenly illuminated. The silhouette of a girl with long, curly hair moved back and forth across the shade.

"What's your roommate's name?" he asked, still looking up at the window.

"Ah, her name's Gretchen," Meg murmured, hating

the ease with which the lies were falling from her lips. "Gretchen Rubin."

"Maybe I can meet her sometime."

"Yeah, maybe." She slid over on the seat and reached for the car door handle.

Meg's hand stopped in midair when she heard the sound of Tim's door opening. She whipped her head around. "What are you doing?"

He already had one foot on the pavement. "I *think* I'm getting out of the car so I can walk you to your door. What does it look like I'm doing?"

Meg bit her lip. It was already time for another lie. "You don't have to do that. I'm a big girl."

Tim leaned forward and gave her a quick kiss on the cheek. "I *want* to. It means a whole extra thirty seconds by your side."

"Well, I have this policy." Her heart constricted painfully inside her chest. "I don't let guys walk me to the door. It's a feminist thing—I'm not some meek lamb who has to be led from place to place. I can get there on my own." Was he going to buy it?

Tim shrugged and looked at her sideways. "Hey, far be it from me to get in the way of women's rights. I'll stay right where I am."

"Thanks." Meg smiled and opened the door. "Maybe someday I can do things your way. But right now there are some personal rules I need to play by."

Meg's walk home had been hurried. Afraid that Tim might drive back to the Vermillion campus for some reason, Meg had stayed in the shadows and kept her eyes peeled for the blue Oldsmobile.

As she unlocked the door to her real home Meg thought about how tricky getting away from Tim had been. *He must have really thought I was weird when I told him I didn't like guys to walk me to the door—I hope he bought my line about women's empowerment.*

Waving good-bye to Tim while making the motions of opening Carman's front door, Meg had been thankful she'd thought to tell Tim that there were strict guidelines about when men could be in the dorms. *I just hope he never makes a surprise visit*, she thought, and crossed her fingers for luck.

"Is that you, honey?" Meg heard her mother's voice as she headed up the stairs to her room.

"Hi, Mom," she yelled, hoping that would be sufficient chit-chat.

Meg could hear her mother's muffled voice calling out something else, but she hurried into her room and shut the door behind her. Even though Tim was worth it, Meg didn't think she could stand to tell one more lie that night.

With the taste of Tim's lips still fresh, Meg wanted to share every delicious detail of the date with Gretchen—the one person with whom she could be completely honest. Punching her friend's number into the telephone, Meg planned the first, tantalizing sentence she would utter once Gretchen picked up the phone.

Unfortunately, it was Mrs. Rubin who answered on the third ring. "Oh, hi, Meg," she said, sounding surprised. "I thought you were with Gretchen."

"No, I, um, had to do something with my parents tonight," Meg answered, biting her lip.

"Well, they all went to a party out at Billy Jenkins's lake house. And Gretchen is sleeping over at Jane's house afterward."

"Thanks, Mrs. Rubin."

Meg hung up the phone quietly and sat on her bed, staring at nothing. Thinking back to lunch on Friday, she had a vague memory of her friends talking about the party. But they hadn't mentioned that they were all spending the night at Jane's, had they?

All of the delicious memories of the night drained out of her and tears welled up in her eyes. *I can't believe they're having a sleepover without me.*

But what did she expect? High school life wasn't going to stop just because Meg no longer wanted to be a part of it. Would she prefer that her best friend sit home on a Saturday night? Of course not.

It's probably better that I don't try to explain Tim to other people, anyway. They'll never be able to understand that this isn't a game to me—it's not something I want to giggle over in homeroom. The way Tim makes me feel is real—so real that it's almost scary. . . .

Five

It rained for the first time in weeks on Monday morning. Meg brushed her teeth and watched fat drops roll down her bathroom window. "I wonder what Tim looks like in the rain," she murmured aloud, enjoying the casual way his name fell off her lips. She imagined him running across the university campus, an old baseball cap his only protection from the weather. She could almost hear the squeaking sound his wet Converse high-tops would make as he walked into class.

Meg zipped the English paper she'd finished Sunday into her backpack. Tramping downstairs for a quick breakfast, she reflected that being in love with Tim had the definite potential to do major damage to her grade-point average. The night before, she'd sworn to herself that she wouldn't let thoughts of Tim break her concentration. But when she'd tried to develop an introductory paragraph about dramatic irony in Shakespeare's *Romeo and Juliet,* images of Tim standing under her balcony, comparing her to the sun, kept floating into her brain.

Of course, I don't have a balcony, Meg thought. *Even if I did, it would be pretty tough for Tim to stand beneath it—considering he has no idea where I really live.* If the mental picture of Tim reciting poetry to an unsuspecting girl in Carman Hall didn't fill Meg with such panic, she would have laughed. It was the kind of situation that Gretchen always found hilarious.

Gretchen.

Waves of guilt swept over Meg when she thought of how she'd avoided her best friend's calls all day Sunday. She'd never done that before. Not even when she'd been furious that Gretchen had danced with the then-love of Meg's life, Ron Miles, at an eighth-grade autumn mixer.

Meg wasn't sure why she didn't feel like talking to Gretchen. Especially because the first thing she'd done when she got home on Saturday was to pick up the phone and dial Gretchen's number. Maybe it was because she'd felt so let down that Gretchen was over at Jane's when Meg had needed her. It was stupid, but Meg felt as if her friends were re-forming into a group that didn't include her. Why hadn't they at least told her about the slumber party—asked her if she wanted to come over after her date?

If she left high school behind for Tim, did that mean high school was going to leave her behind, too?

●　　　●　　　●

Rain seemed to have invaded Southwest High School. Damp pieces of spiral-notebook paper clung to the cool tiled floors, and a dripping windbreaker hung from the back of nearly every chair. Teachers had umbrellas propped up in the corners of their classrooms. The umbrellas' sturdy handles and sharp tips were a steady reminder of what lay outside the fluorescent world of the school building.

Meg fought off the rainy-day blahs by staring out the window and reliving the moment when Tim had traced his calloused thumb along the line of her jawbone. Rather than take notes about the *x* factor during Mr. Hannigan's Algebra II class, Meg savored the way Tim had mouthed good-bye to her once she'd closed his car door.

She was vaguely aware that Mr. Hannigan was passing out worksheets and shouting hurried instructions while students gathered their books and stampeded out the door on their way to lunch. *I didn't even hear the bell ring,* she realized. *I guess I'm turning into a full-time daydreamer.* She thought wryly that pretty soon she was going to find herself drawing hearts with Tim's initials in them all over the margins of her notebook.

Meg's thoughts broke off abruptly when she experienced the familiar sensation of Gretchen falling into step beside her.

"Hey, Henry, let's speed up the walk to lunch. It's pizza today, and you know that in this school *pepperoni* is synonymous with *madhouse*." Gretchen reached over and gave Meg's ponytail her signature tug.

"Hi, Gretch."

"Where were you yesterday? I was waiting by the phone for the latest segment of *Megan Henry: Now a Hit TV Miniseries.*"

"I had to write a paper for Quigly's class."

"Ever heard of study breaks? They're this awesome invention that a disgruntled teenager of the nineteen-fifties thought up."

"Ha, ha." Meg tried not to smile, but her record for resisting the temptation to laugh at Gretchen's jokes was just under five minutes.

"Come on, Meggie. Why didn't you want to talk?"

"You know I hate it when you call me that."

"I had to get your attention somehow." Gretchen shrugged. "I was beginning to think you got a severe head injury this weekend—one that rendered you unable to communicate with your best friend."

"I just thought you'd be tired after staying up late with Jane and Maria on Saturday. Your *mom* informed me that you all were spending the night together."

"Is that why you're riled? Because I spent the night at Jane's without you?"

When Gretchen put it that way, Meg realized that her anger was pretty childish. Still, she couldn't help clinging to it—if she admitted to herself that Gretchen hadn't done anything wrong, she'd have to justify her reluctance to give away the details of her day with Tim.

"I'm *riled,* as you say, because you didn't even tell me that you were going over there," Meg stated, opting to continue attacking in lieu of a good defense.

"What should I have done?" Gretchen asked. "Called you up on Tim's car phone and said, 'Yo, Meg, I'm going over to Jane's now'?"

"Tim doesn't have a car phone." Meg felt her argument weakening. Within minutes, she was going to have to come out with a full apology. *Why am I such a total jerk sometimes?* she asked herself.

"You get the point," Gretchen said.

"Yeah, I get it. I guess I overreacted a little, huh?"

"Just a little," Gretchen responded, holding her thumb and index finger an inch apart.

"Friends?"

"Definitely." Gretchen threw her arm around Meg's shoulder. "On one condition," she continued, giving Meg a friendly squeeze.

"What's that?" Meg asked.

"You tell me all the juicy details about Saturday—including an estimation of how many minutes were actually spent lip to lip."

"That sounds like an offer I can't refuse."

"You said it, not me."

Now that she wasn't mad, Meg felt a fresh rush of guilt over not telling Gretchen about the incredible time she'd had with Tim. Until recently she'd shared every detail of her life with Gretchen. But it was getting harder to mesh the two sides of her life—the one with family and friends, and the other with Tim— without feeling like a total hypocrite. Her existence had sort of become like the physics theory about split universes: she was simultaneously living in more than one time and place. Of course, eventually she'd have to choose which world she really belonged in.

In the meantime, she'd tell Gretchen all about

Tim. *If I don't at least try to communicate what I'm going through to Gretchen, something in our friendship is going to be lost. And I can't have that happen—she's too important to me.*

As Meg hurried through campus the university library loomed ahead; its huge domed roof stood out against the twilight sky in high relief. *The place is a fortress,* Meg thought. *How does anyone find a book in a place that huge?*

After three long days without Tim, knowing that she was just moments from being with him again made Meg's heart pound. She wiped her moist palms on her mint-green sundress and shifted the weight of the books in her arms. Part of her nervousness was left over from the lie she'd told her parents not half an hour before.

"I'm going to the library tonight with Gretchen," she'd explained at dinner.

"Are you two working on a project together?" Mrs. Henry had asked.

Meg hadn't thought that far ahead; she'd hesitated a beat too long before responding. "Uh, yeah, we are."

"What class is it for?"

Meg had had her parents' full attention. *This is why everybody needs a sibling,* she thought. *Distraction.*

"History," Meg had blurted. It was then that her palms had started sweating. Would her parents be suspicious if she collapsed from severe heart palpitations?

"I thought Gretchen had Ms. Gorman for history."

"Oh, she does. I meant that we're both *starting* history projects—different ones—so we thought we might as well go to the library together." Meg had crossed her fingers in her lap. She'd prayed her mother would let the subject drop.

"Call if you're going to be later than ten o'clock."

Meg had let out a huge sigh of relief. Not trusting her voice, she'd begun shoving food mechanically into her mouth.

Meg saw Tim waiting at the library entrance. *At least I really am going to a library*, Meg assured herself. *Just a different library with a different person.* That hardly qualified as a major lie—it was more in the small-fib category.

As she skipped up the last steps in front of the library Tim turned with a dazzling smile. His hair looked like it was wet from a shower, and he had an old backpack draped casually over one shoulder. A flush of pleasure spread across Meg's cheeks, and her grin was so wide she thought her face might break.

Tim put his arms around Meg's waist and brushed his lips lightly over hers. A warm tingle traveled down her spine.

"Hi there," she greeted him shyly.

"Hi yourself." Tim put an arm around Meg's shoulders and guided her into the enormous marble lobby of Rosedale Library. "I was watching you charge across campus. You looked like you were pretty deep in thought."

"I was."

"Care to expand on that?" Tim led Meg to a large carrell in the back of the main reading room.

"Maybe when I know you better," Meg answered, glancing up at the perfect line of Tim's jaw from beneath her eyelashes. She was always amazed by how easy it was to flirt and be bold with Tim. It was sort of like bungee jumping. One minute Meg was standing at the edge of a cliff, her feet firmly on familiar ground. Then all of a sudden she was hurtling through space over rushing water. At that point, the only thing to do was to spread her arms wide open and embrace the danger.

"Is the library at Vermillion a good place to study?" Tim was asking.

"Oh, yeah, it's fine. Very quiet." Meg stopped herself from improvising details about nonexistent stained-glass windows and cozy lamp-lit reading rooms. She made a mental note to check out the Vermillion library so that she'd be more prepared if the subject came up again. There was so much to keep track of.

Tim and Meg settled into their chairs, books and notepads spread before them. Meg had brought the novel she was reading for English. Earlier that evening she'd run the list of her other textbooks through her mind: *French II For High School*, *Algebra II For Beginners*, *Tenth-Grade World History*. Not exactly suitable for a college curriculum. Algebra factors could wait until homeroom, she had decided.

Meg pulled out her paperback copy of Jonathan Swift's *Gulliver's Travels*. She got into her standard reading position, her legs propped up on the chair across from her, and tried to concentrate on Gulliver's journey to the land of the Lilliputians. The words of the novel swam before her eyes, the letters running together like black watercolor paint.

Tim's leg was next to hers, so close that Meg could feel the heat of his body. *I will read*, Meg told herself. *But first I need to see what Tim looks like when he's studying.*

She glanced at Tim sideways, her face still bent toward the book in her hands. In a heartbeat, she found herself gazing straight into Tim's dark blue eyes. They both jerked back quickly. The sound of Tim's notebook falling with a thud onto the wood table boomed through the silent library.

At least twenty heads swiveled in their direction. Meg's face heated up, and she smiled sheepishly. As Tim bent to retrieve his pen she heard his soft laughter.

"I guess we caught each other staring," he said.

"I think the entire library caught us staring." Meg felt the urge to giggle, and she quickly put a hand over her mouth.

Tim gently pried Meg's fingers from her lips and brought his face to within just inches of hers. "I wouldn't want to disappoint our adoring fans by not giving them a show," he breathed against her ear.

The touch of Tim's lips against her earlobe, then her neck, blotted out Meg's awareness of her surroundings. She closed her eyes and reveled in the sensation of being near Tim. A sharp whistle brought her back to reality, and she drew back, embarrassed.

"I think we've outstayed our welcome," Tim whispered.

Meg nodded. Tim arched his eyebrows quirkily and gave her a goofy smile, evoking fresh waves of laughter from her.

"Let's go out on the steps for a while," he continued, running his index finger down her forearm.

Meg followed Tim through the maze of tables, conscious of several girls' envious stares. She wasn't thrilled about making a scene in the library, but she was proud of being with Tim. *I bet there are at least ten girls in here who would love to switch places with me*, she thought.

Outside, the sun was setting over the rolling hills of the campus. Streams of students spilled over the brick paths that led from building to building. Under huge oak trees, couples lounged in the grass, talking and laughing. Meg relished the thought that she and Tim were among those who'd been lured away from schoolwork by the romance of the fresh spring evening.

Meg sat down next to Tim on one of the wide walls that bordered the steps of the library. The stone was still warm from the afternoon sun, and Meg leaned back on her elbows. A feeling of contentment drifted through her.

"When you asked me out for a study date, you should have emphasized the date part," she joked.

"It's true that we haven't gotten much done in the way of academics," Tim conceded. He maneuvered his body so that he could lie down and rest his head on one of Meg's knees. His wavy hair tickled the soft skin of her leg.

"But I'm studying right now," he went on.

"Oh, yeah? What are you studying?" Meg asked, noticing the sunlight glistening on his black hair.

"How you look upside down. I think I'll write a paper on your face for my Twentieth-Century Aesthetics class."

Meg's heart fluttered. She marveled at how every little thing that Tim said to her seemed to change her body temperature. *Billy Jenkins couldn't have this effect on me in a million years.*

Tim pulled Meg's head down and kissed her on the forehead. When she looked up again, Meg saw Gloria and Laurie staring at her from the other side of the steps. From the open-mouthed expressions on their faces, it was clear that Caroline's bridesmaids were surprised to see her. *Oh, no,* Meg groaned inwardly. *They're going to say something!*

"Meg, what are you doing here?" Gloria called as she strode over to the wall where Tim and Meg were sitting.

"Tim and I were in the library." Meg pleaded with her eyes, begging Gloria and Laurie to maintain her cover.

"I coaxed Meg off the Vermillion campus," Tim added. He placed a possessive arm around her shoulder.

"Vermillion *College?*" Laurie asked.

"Of course, Laurie," Gloria interjected. "You remember that illustrious women's college that's practically right next door?"

Meg breathed a sigh of relief. Gloria was going to cover for her.

"I know what Vermillion *is*," Laurie continued. "I just don't understand what connection it has to—"

"Tim and I should really get back to the library," Meg interrupted. She could hear the edge in her voice.

"We'll catch you guys later," Gloria said, tugging on Laurie's arm.

"Nice seeing you," Tim called to the girls' retreating figures.

Meg stood up, willing her hands to stop shaking. At the base of the library steps, Gloria turned back around and raised her eyebrows. Meg could see disapproval written all over her face.

Meg had been lucky that time. But what was going to happen the next time? And the next?

"Laurie seems a little out of it," Tim observed. "Why did she have such a strange reaction to Vermillion, anyway?"

"Maybe she wasn't happy to see you and me together," Meg answered lightly. "I got the impression at Caroline's wedding that she has sort of a crush on you."

Tim threw his head back and laughed. "Right," he said. "A college senior with a freshman nobody. Like that would ever be a possibility."

"Stranger things have happened," Meg answered.

I can't tell him the truth, she realized. *Not now— maybe not ever.*

Six

"TGIF," Gretchen shouted. She threw her backpack at Meg's feet and sat down next to her.

"Think about the word *Friday*," Meg said to Gretchen. "When the English language was evolving, I wonder if anyone knew that one day kids all across the world would get giddy at the sound of that word."

Shady Park was full of students from Southwest High. Directly across from the high school, the small park was a place famous for breaking up, making up, and making out—not always in that order. Perched on the side of the fountain at the center of the green, Meg and Gretchen could hear ten different Friday-night plans being formulated, discussed, and discarded.

"More importantly, did they know that we'd get a knot in our stomachs when the words *date to the junior prom* were put in one sentence?" Gretchen responded.

"Gretch, I really hope you're not already stressing about going to the junior prom."

"It's only a few weeks away. Besides, if I worry now, maybe it'll be out of my system by the time I have to sit home alone while every other sophomore girl is dancing till dawn under the leftover Christmas-tree lights from the winter dance I didn't get invited to."

"The winter dance was boring. David Arnold spent the whole night telling me about his boygenius PSAT scores." Meg stuck out her tongue at the memory. Then she smiled, remembering how she'd fantasized that she was dancing with Tim instead of David.

"That's still better than watching the colorized version of *Miracle on 34th Street* with your family."

"Well, I, for one, will not be going to the junior prom," Meg announced.

"Why not?"

"Does the name Tim Wilson ring a bell? He's not exactly going to ask me to the Southwest junior prom!"

"What if you guys break up by then?"

"Gretchen! Don't say that."

"What if some innocent bystander tells him the truth?"

"First of all, I *am* going to tell him about my age—soon."

"And you think he's going to laugh it off when and if—I'm emphasizing the *if*—you 'fess up?"

"I don't know what'll happen," Meg said miserably. Gretchen's eternal pragmatism was threatening to ruin her Friday afternoon.

"Meg, I'm not trying to be a jerk. I just don't want to see this thing crush you."

"How is being in love going to crush me?"

"Be realistic. What kind of future does this relationship have? It's based on a lie, and every day you dig yourself in deeper. Eventually the dishonesty is going to explode in your face."

"Since when are you a pop psychologist?" Meg asked.

"Since my best friend started needing one." Gretchen's solemn expression made Meg's heart drop.

"My life would be so much simpler if Tim were in high school," Meg sighed.

"If Tim were in high school, you probably wouldn't want to date him," Gretchen pointed out.

"What's that supposed to mean?"

"Come on, Meg. You've said a dozen times that the reason Tim is so great is because he's mature—unlike our beloved guys at Southwest."

"So?"

"So he wasn't born that way. I'm sure Tim did the same stupid stuff that Billy Jenkins does now. You've just caught him when he's ripe."

"Tim's not a piece of fruit, Gretch."

Gretchen rolled her eyes. "Okay. Let's just say he's gotten better with age—like a bottle of fine wine."

"All right, maybe part of the reason I like Tim so much *is* because he's in college. Big deal!"

"Meg, the idea is that this chemistry—or kismet, or whatever you want to call this thing between you and Tim—*is* a big deal. That's why you have to think about consequences."

"Now you sound like a health teacher."

"If you're planning to throw away your whole high school career for a guy, you've got to consider all the implications."

"Who the heck said anything about throwing away my whole high school career?"

"Not two minutes ago, you told me you weren't going to the junior prom."

"I'd hardly say one prom adds up to four years of living."

"Just wait. Today you're skipping a dance. Tomorrow you might be ditching your own graduation ceremony in favor of a frat party."

Tim doesn't even like frat parties, Meg said to herself. But it wasn't the moment to discuss her growing list of Tim Wilson trivia. She needed a favor from Gretchen.

"If I cross my heart and hope to die that I won't skip out on caps and gowns for *any* reason, then can I ask you for a tiny favor?"

"How tiny?" Gretchen looked skeptical.

"Just cover for me tonight if my mom happens to call your house looking for me."

"You and loverboy have a hot date?"

Meg nodded.

"I'll do it," Gretchen relented. "But don't think this means I condone the way you're lying to the poor guy."

Gretchen's words barely registered. With that problem taken care of, Meg was staring into space, already debating whether to choose jeans or a miniskirt for the jazz concert. She turned to get a second opinion.

"Gretch, should I wear—" Meg stopped. She was alone at the fountain. Gretchen had left without a word.

At dusk, Meg strolled through Elysian Field, the big lawn surrounding the community center. She spotted Tim to the left of the makeshift stage, where four musicians were tuning their instruments. Tim had spread a large checkered sheet on the grass, and beside him was a Styrofoam cooler.

Meg approached him from the back, sneaking up quietly so that she could cover Tim's eyes with one hand. "Guess who?" she asked.

Before she could even take a breath, Tim grasped her hand and pulled her into his lap. She struggled to sit up, but Tim threw one of his strong legs over both of hers. With his hands, he grabbed the back of her head and held it in place. Meg gasped with pleasure as Tim's lips found hers.

The kiss was long and searching. Meg twined her fingers in Tim's hair, trying to get closer. His mouth moved to her eyelids, fluttering gently against her long lashes.

"How did you know it was me?" she murmured.

Tim moved his head slightly away from hers. "Meg, is that you? Oops. I thought you were the lemonade vendor."

Meg rolled off his lap and took a swat at his chest. "Very funny. I happen to have noticed that the guy selling lemonade has a bushy mustache and a hairy chest—not your type at all."

"Actually, I saw you the second you walked onto the field. I watched you make your way through the crowd, edging closer and closer to my little oasis."

"Why didn't you call out to me?"

"I don't know. I just wanted those few minutes to spy on you. It was like seeing you in a movie or something."

Tim's voice was teasing, but his gaze was intent. Meg was intoxicated by the idea that Tim had felt the same fascination from afar that she'd experienced from the bleachers at soccer games. Still, Gretchen's warnings rang in her ears.

What if someone from school had been there? Tim would have wanted to know why Meg had stopped to talk to a group of boys who were squirting water through their teeth—or doing something even more inane. She groaned inwardly. *I have to watch every move I make.*

"Do you make a habit of spying on unsuspecting women?" Meg finally asked.

"Nah. Just the ones I find intriguing."

"Is that a long list?"

"Nope. The name Megan Henry is first and last."

Meg closed her eyes as the mellow sound of the saxophone drifted through the night air. She was full from the picnic dinner Tim had prepared, and she was lying back, her head resting on one folded arm.

"You make a mean picnic," Meg commented.

"Thanks, but I can't take all the credit," Tim said, lacing his fingers through Meg's. "The university dining service helped me out," he continued. "I swiped most of the food from the all-you-can-eat cafeteria."

"Really?" Meg pictured Tim stuffing apples and cookies into his backpack.

"Yeah. The food's pretty good there. I hear Vermillion has a soda machine. That must be nice."

"It must be— I mean, it is." Meg cursed herself for the near slip-up. Of course she should know about the dining hall at Vermillion.

Music from a trumpet and a stand-up bass joined the saxophone. Each musician took a turn performing solo; the audience clapped appreciatively as each finished his turn. Tim seemed absorbed in the rhythm of the music.

"Hey, this is an old Billie Holiday classic," he said suddenly.

Meg nodded. " 'Let's Do It,' " she responded.

"Do you mean that?" Tim's eyes twinkled as he ran a hand over her bare calf.

"I was referring to the name of the song."

"I didn't realize you were such a jazz connoisseur."

"I'm not, really. But there's something in Billie Holiday's voice that gets to me. She's so sad, but at the same time so strong. It's like she's two people at once." Meg's voice trailed off. *Am I really talking about music?* she wondered.

"And that speaks to you?" Tim's voice was quiet.

"Sure. I mean, the notion that there are two parts to every person is everywhere. Think about Jekyll and Hyde, Dr. Frankenstein and the monster, Luke Skywalker and Darth Vader. They're all two sides to one being."

"Is there another Meg? One I can't see?"

Meg looked away from Tim. "Yes." Her answer was a whisper in the darkness.

Tim held Meg's left hand, his fingers delicately tracing the lines of her palm. "I've never met a woman like you," he said.

"Is that good or bad?"

"The best." Time stood still as Tim took Meg in his arms.

He didn't kiss her. He held her in a tight hug, his hands running up and down the length of her spine. The concert music mingled with the breeze, washing over them.

"There might be conflicting lives going on inside of us both," Tim said. "But right now our hearts are beating together."

Meg held her breath and listened for the sound of her heart. It was true. Their hearts were thumping in unison. *Someday,* she promised silently, *I'll tell you all about the other Megan Henry.*

They left Tim's car radio off during the drive back to the dorm. The sounds from the jazz concert still echoed in Meg's ears, lulling her to sleep.

"We're here." Tim's voice broke into Meg's drowsy haze. She looked out the window, half expecting to see the tidy lawn in front of her house. Instead, Carman Hall stood like a sealed fortress before her.

"Don't wait," she said hastily. "I have to go around back."

"Why?"

"I, uh, accidentally left a library book outside. I need to grab it."

Tim hesitated.

He's trying to be a gentleman, and I'm not letting him, Meg realized. Guilt sat in her stomach like a rock. "It's okay. Really," she added.

"Good night, then." Tim's tone held an edge of hurt.

"Sweet dreams." Meg leaned over and kissed him on the lips, letting one hand rest on his knee. "It's sort of hard to say good-bye."

Tim pulled her close for a more lingering kiss. "Meg, I meant it when I said I've never met anyone like you before."

"I just hope you never regret having met me at all." Meg jumped out of the car before Tim had a chance to respond. When she was halfway up the lawn in front of the dorm, she turned and blew him a kiss. Meg stood still until she saw Tim's tail lights fade into the night.

Out of breath and sweating from her jog home, Meg peeked through the family-room window at the front of her house. Mrs. Henry was curled up on the sofa in her bathrobe, watching an old black-and-white movie on television. Meg pushed the light button on her digital watch for the tenth time since Tim had dropped her off. *Oh, no,* she groaned inwardly. She was twenty-five minutes late for curfew. *Please, Mom, be in a good mood— or better yet, asleep.*

Meg crossed her fingers and unlocked the front

door as quietly as was humanly possible. She felt like a burglar. *Can you get arrested for breaking and entering into your own home?* she wondered. She started to tiptoe up the stairs.

"Meg!" Mrs. Henry sounded wide awake.

"Hi, Mom. What're you doing up?"

"Funny. I was going to ask you the same question." Mrs. Henry patted the space next to her on the couch. There was no choice but to sit down.

Let this be short and relatively painless, Meg prayed. "I'm sorry I'm late. Gretchen and I—"

"Before you go into lengthy explanations that may or may not be true, let's get something straight."

This doesn't sound good, Meg thought. "Sure. What?" She didn't pull off nonchalance exactly, but she managed not to stutter.

"I have an instinct that your being late doesn't have anything to do with Gretchen."

Meg's picnic dinner threatened to force its way out of her body. "You do?" she gulped.

"Yes." Mrs. Henry paused for a moment. "I don't want you to think I try to snoop into your private life—I know you have a mind of your own. But I hear you talking on the phone, and I can't help but gather bits of information."

"And?" Meg knew she shouldn't encourage her mother to continue, but she couldn't stop herself. She felt as if she were experiencing free fall, and all she wanted to do was hit bottom as quickly as possible.

"Well, I have a suspicion that a certain older boy is keeping you out past curfew."

Meg's legs went numb. "Oh," she whispered.

"I know Billy Jenkins is a hot shot at school," Mrs. Henry continued. "I've heard you and Gretchen giggling about him for years. But at your age a year can make a big difference. I think you probably catch the gist of what I'm saying?"

Meg's respiratory system started working again. "Don't worry, Mom. I've got everything under control."

"Ease up on the brakes, Meg. If there's one thing that'll make a driver nasty, it's seeing the car in front riding the brakes."

Meg gripped the steering wheel tighter. *Millions of people drive cars,* she told herself. *This should be a piece of cake.*

Her father continued with his instructions. "Always go the speed of traffic."

Meg nodded mutely.

"Remember to use your blinker."

"I know."

"Okay, let's take this ramp onto the highway."

"Are you sure I'm ready for it?" Meg reluctantly inched onto the freeway. Four lanes of traffic sounded like a death sentence.

"Positive."

Meg settled back into the driver's seat. She could see miles of cars ahead, all speeding off to separate destinations. It was actually kind of fun. She had a ton of steel at her whim.

"Feeling better?" Mr. Henry asked cheerfully.

Meg took her eyes off the road for just a second to look at her dad. "I feel great. It's like there are no limits to where I could go. This definitely beats a ten-speed."

"It's hard to believe that in a few weeks you'll be a licensed driver. And then pretty soon you'll grad-uate, go to college, start a career—"

"Dad, please. Don't get all nostalgic on me."

"Sorry. But ever since Caroline's wedding you've seemed so grown-up. I don't know why I never realized it before."

Meg bit her lip and blinked back a tear. It was like her parents had some high-tech radar that alerted them that something inside her was chang-ing. She knew that the only way to make her plague of guilt go away was to tell them the truth. But things were different from when she'd been young and could confess any bad deed to her par-ents. Going out with a college guy wasn't on a par with eating a cookie before dinner, or borrowing her mother's jewelry without permission. If she came clean about Tim, her whole relationship with her parents would be tarnished. For freedom, she'd have to give up the purity of childhood.

But Tim was worth the awful deception. Every minute with him was worth an hour, even a year, of guilt and confusion. And weren't all of her horri-ble, mixed-up emotions a part of growing up? *If only I could make everyone understand,* she thought. *I'm not a little girl anymore.*

Seven

"What'd you think?" Gretchen asked on Saturday night as she and Meg left the packed movie theater.

"If you base your opinion of a movie on how many cars the lead guy blows up, I give it a ten."

"Hey, that's what I was going to say!"

"Once again, you and I prove the age-old theory true, Fetchin' Gretchen."

"What theory is that?"

"Great minds think alike!"

Meg and Gretchen walked through the mall in companionable silence. The unspoken tension of the last few weeks faded into the background of neon signs and trendy boutiques. Meg was happy to let the subject of her clandestine romance with Tim drop for the night. Between her mom's weird talk with her the night before and her dad's trip down memory lane that morning, she felt like being young, innocent, and guilt-free for a few hours.

"Not that I'm complaining, but you still haven't told me where Tim the Great is tonight," Gretchen said, breaking the silence.

"He's away at a track meet." *So much for avoiding the topic of Tim,* Meg thought.

"Am I going to be privy to any scenes from next week's tantalizing episode of *Meg and Tim: A May-December Romance for the Nineties?*"

"Would you settle for a commercial break?"

"Uh-oh. Don't tell me there's trouble in paradise."

"Not trouble exactly. I think Tim is more wonderful every time I see him. But—"

"Let me guess. You've decided he's too young for you? Maybe you've fallen in love with his philosophy professor?"

"Gretchen!"

"Wait, I've got it. You're in love with his philosophy professor, and you've convinced the sucker that you're a graduate student!" Gretchen twirled around, clasping her hands in front of her heart.

"If you don't shut up, I'm going to buy a soft-serve ice cream and shove it up your nose."

"Now that you mention it, I *am* a little hungry. Let's see who's loafing around the food court."

"I'll buy fries, you buy a shake," Meg answered. At least hanging out at the crowded food court would thwart Gretchen's questions.

They sat down at a small wrought-iron table. Despite the high roof covering the whole area, the mall owners apparently had thought it would be cute to put umbrellas over the tables. Eating there was somewhere between going to a snack bar at Disney World and having dinner at a futuristic bubble community on Mars.

"I'll get the food, you guard our stuff," Meg said as she took off toward Michael's Munchies on the other side of the court.

Meg trod her way back to the table cautiously. Chocolate shake drippings ran over the edge of the tray onto her hand. She was so intent on balancing the food that she didn't notice someone had joined Gretchen at their table.

"I went for the gold and got cheese fries—" Meg stopped in midsentence.

"Hey, Meg." Billy Jenkins's lazy drawl caught her off guard.

"Billy! What's up?" Meg took in Billy's long, jean-clad legs, black motorcycle boots, and over-confident expression. *He really thinks he's God's gift!* she thought.

"I was just telling Gretchen that I bought a car today." Billy's green eyes flickered from Meg to Gretchen.

"It's an old Fiat convertible," Gretchen added.

"Wow! You must be psyched," Meg responded. She raised her eyebrows as Billy sat down at their small table. He was such a typical guy. When she didn't have a boyfriend, he wouldn't give her the time of day; now he was hanging out with her on Saturday night.

Meg dropped into the chair next to Billy's. She propped one slim ankle on the table and leaned back with the chocolate shake in her hand. Having the advantage for a change felt good. Part of her hoped that Billy would suffer a little when he found out she was dating Tim. Actually, most of her hoped so.

As if on cue, Billy gave Meg a half grin. "I haven't seen you around much, Meg. Don't tell me your mom grounded you for getting straight *A*s."

"Not quite. I've been busy."

Billy rested one bent leg on the iron armrest of Gretchen's chair.

"She's got a boyfriend," Gretchen interjected.

"Oh, yeah? Cool."

Cool wasn't the reaction she'd hoped for. Billy didn't have to tear out his hair and jump on a funeral pyre, but he could at least have the decency to look uncomfortable!

"So you must be pretty happy about having your own set of wheels." *His own set of wheels?* Meg's words reverberated in her brain. She decided she sounded like someone out of a bad 1950s sitcom.

"I am." Billy glanced briefly in Meg's direction, then turned his gaze back to Gretchen. "So, Gretch, when do you get your license?"

"Not for a couple of months, actually."

"Maybe I could teach you to drive this summer."

"Would you? That would be great!" Gretchen's face had gone a little pink, and she was tugging on one earlobe—a sure sign she was nervous.

"Do you want a ride home?" Billy asked.

Meg was feeling like the Invisible Woman. First driving lessons, next a ride home. Billy's question hadn't been that friendly "Hey, do you guys need a ride a home—it's no problem" type of question. It had definitely fallen into the "I've been thinking about asking you on a date so I'll offer you a ride home and ask on the way" category. And the offer hadn't been to Meg.

"Well, Meg and I are here together. We were going to get my mom to pick us up. . . ." Gretchen's voice wavered a little.

"No problem. Meg can jump in the back. The car's a two-seater, but there's a space for suitcases and stuff."

Wonderful, Meg thought. *I've been relegated to Billy Jenkins's luggage compartment.*

"Meg?" Gretchen's voice was brimming with hope.

"Sounds good." Meg stared at the glob of ketchup at the bottom of the plate of french fries. She had to remember that she was in love with Tim. She shouldn't care about some stupid drive in Billy's new car.

The bright green Fiat stood out from the other cars in the parking lot. In a sea of gray, powder-blue, and maroon familymobiles, the little convertible was a symbol of freedom. Billy didn't bother opening his door. He hopped into the driver's seat and revved the engine.

Wedging into the space between the front seats and the trunk was an effort. Meg's knees were up to her chin; she gripped one side of the car for balance.

"Are you okay back there, Meg?" Billy asked while Gretchen settled herself into the passenger-side bucket seat.

"Fine." A corner of Billy's history textbook sent

shooting pains through Meg's lower back. When she reached under her to shove it out of the way, a page ripped in her hand. She looked down between her legs. *Oops!*

"I hope page forty-two isn't going to be on your next history test," Meg said to the back of Billy's head.

He turned to look at her. "Why?"

Gretchen leaned over and followed Meg's eyes to the crumpled pages of the book.

"Never mind," Meg mumbled.

"Are we ready?" Gretchen asked quickly.

Billy threw the car into reverse. He peeled out of the parking lot, turning the radio up to full volume. Gretchen leaned back and laughed into the wind.

Tuesday evening Meg pedaled through her neighborhood, speeding past a blur of houses and trees. She barely paused at stop signs; in her head she counted down the minutes until Tim would show up at Carman Hall to pick her up for the movie.

Four more blocks.

Two more.

Finally Carman Hall came into view. Tim's Oldsmobile was nowhere in sight. Meg jumped off her bike and wheeled it over to the stand in front of the dorm. Two girls threw a Frisbee back and forth across the lawn. Another strummed an acoustic guitar.

She'd have to be sure not to cut it that close again. If Tim had gotten a chance to talk to those girls, the inevitable "do you know . . . ?" round of questions would have started. How could she explain that none of her dormmates had ever heard of her?

When Tim pulled up to the curb, Meg jumped in the car. The smell of old leather and Tim's shampoo filled the front seat.

"Hi!" Meg fastened her seat belt.

"Hey. You didn't have to wait out front," Tim greeted her. "I could have come to the door."

"That's okay." Meg smiled.

Tim slid over to Meg's side of the car and put his hands on her shoulders. His kiss tasted of toothpaste.

"Crest or Colgate?" she asked.

"Aim."

"I like it."

"Thanks, ma'am. I 'aim' to please."

Meg groaned. "Your jokes remind me of my dad's."

"They say a girl always falls for a younger version of her father, so I'll take that as a compliment."

Meg tossed her purse into the back seat. It fell on top of a heap of Tim's track clothes, books, and assorted junk. *I'll take Tim's comfy four-door over Billy's flashy two-seater any day,* she thought. The Oldsmobile was a safe haven. As long as they were driving, she was alone with Tim and away from prying eyes.

"So, what movie are we going to?"

"We have two choices—either a critically acclaimed French film at the Fine Arts Theater, or a Stephen King movie at the Sixty-fourth Street drive-in." Tim handed her the movie listings from the newspaper. "Take your pick."

"Hmm . . . I do love subtitles. I mean, *La Dolce Vita* was amazing."

"True." Tim took his eyes off the road and smiled at her.

"On the other hand, a drive-in can be a great learning experience."

"Enlighten me."

"The drive-in is like a history lesson. Old-time American culture at its best. If we were living thirty years ago, going to the drive-in would be automatic." Meg paused. "Not to mention the people-watching we could do there."

"There's another good reason to go to the Stephen King movie," Tim added. "We won't have any armrests between us."

Meg blushed. He'd seen right through her bogus reasons for wanting to stay in the car. The truth was, two hours parked in a dark lot sounded incredibly appealing. Almost too appealing.

It was barely dark when they pulled up in front of the huge screen. The tops of tall trees poked up behind the screen, and the sky provided an indigo-blue backdrop. Under the moon and bright clusters of stars, the gaudy images of the theater's concession-stand advertisement were surreal. The jumbo pop-corn container on the screen must have been twenty feet tall.

A smattering of cars dotted the parking lot. In front of them, a man in overalls was spreading a blanket over the flat part of his pickup truck, which he'd pulled in backward. To the side, a little girl was walking toward her mother with a teetering stack of soda cups and candy boxes.

"Let's load up on junk food before the movie starts," Tim suggested. "I'll be right back." He got out of the car and bounded toward the concession stand.

Meg pulled down Tim's vanity mirror and stared at her reflection. Would Tim believe she was in college if he'd just met her that night? She'd been in such a hurry after doing errands with her mom that she hadn't bothered with half the makeup that she usually applied before seeing Tim. And she'd had to leave her hair pulled back in the red scrunchie she'd worn all day at school. Still, there was something in her eyes that made her look older. *Being in love must speed up the aging process,* Meg thought.

"Are you the fairest of them all?"

Meg jumped at Tim's voice. She hastily snapped the mirror back in place.

"I thought I had something in my eye," she said.

"Really?"

Meg laughed. "No."

"Anytime you want to know how beautiful you look, just ask me." Tim tucked a loose strand of ash-blond hair behind her ear.

"Enough flattery. Give me food." Bantering with Tim was confusing. The part of her that traded witty remarks was calm and collected—but the part that had been studying her reflection in the mirror agonized over every word.

"You do look different tonight," Tim mused. He opened a bag of Twizzlers and absently tied one into a knot.

"I do?" Why had she fixated on that dumb mirror? She might as well have put a sign on her forehead that said Examine Me for Flaws.

"Yeah. You look more . . . innocent than usual."

Uh-oh. "Probably because my hair's in a pony-tail," Meg said.

"Hmm. Maybe . . ."

It was like being on a microscope slide. If he guessed the truth, should she confess? Or flat-out lie?

"Anyway," Tim continued, "you look great—as usual." He wrapped his arms around her. "You know what's coming up this weekend?"

Meg narrowed her eyes. "Another out-of-state track meet?"

"Try again."

"The national bowling championships?"

"Don't tease me. It's our one-month anniversary, and you know it."

She knew it, all right. It was practically all she thought about. She'd been lying to Tim for a month, and she still couldn't think of a good way to tell him the truth.

She almost wished she didn't like him so much. If he'd had some terrible flaw, then she could have broken it off, and Tim would never have to know the truth. But he didn't have any terrible flaws. As far as she could tell, he was about as perfect as a guy could be.

"We've known each other almost four weeks. It's gone by so fast, I feel like I haven't had a chance to tell you a lot of things about me," Meg said cautiously.

"Don't worry. Eventually I'll find out everything. Every last detail." He held her close and kissed the top of her head.

Meg snuggled against his chest, grateful that the movie credits were beginning to roll across the screen.

• • •

It wasn't quite ten-thirty when Meg biked into her family's garage. Her parents were at the kitchen table doing a crossword puzzle together.

"Name a New Jersey town," Mr. Henry said. "Four letters."

"How was the baseball game?" her mother asked.

"Fun." Meg looked over her father's shoulder at the clues. "Thirty-seven across is *ripe*," she said.

"Good job," Mr. Henry said, filling in the letters. "Who won?"

"We did." *At least there's a fifty-fifty chance we did.*

"Your phone was ringing off the hook, so we finally answered it," Mrs. Henry said.

"Who was it?"

"Gretchen."

"Thanks. I'll call her."

Mrs. Henry put a bag of popcorn into the microwave. "I thought you said you were going to the game with Gretchen."

"She ended up having to baby-sit. I went with Maria."

"Oh."

The room was quiet except for the hum of the microwave and the popping sounds of exploding kernels of popcorn. Meg looked blankly at her mother, who was staring at her with unspoken questions.

"I think I'll go to bed," Meg said to the cabinet above her mother's right shoulder.

• • • •

Meg woke with a start. Her bedroom was still dark; a soft breeze fluttered her curtains. She sat up, her heart pounding.

The kaleidoscopic images of her dream played themselves over in her mind as she made her way to the bathroom.

The dream had been like a videotape on fast forward. First she and Tim had been back at the drive-in, kissing fervently as a housewife was murdered onscreen. In the next segment they'd been lying on Meg's bed. She'd thought it was a room in Carman Hall, until Tim had suddenly demanded to know why she had teddy bears on her shelves and her ninth-grade class picture taped to her mirror.

Before she could come up with a decent excuse, someone had started pounding at her door. "Meg!" her parents were yelling as she'd scrambled off the bed.

Tim had ignored her frantic gestures to climb out of the open window. He'd stood with his mouth agape. Her lips had moved, but no words would come out. As hard as she tried, there'd been no way to explain what she'd done.

Her parents had burst into the room. Face to face with Tim, her mother had started crying. A million different accusations had flown at Meg. She'd crumpled to the floor, sobbing.

Now, awake, Meg stood at her bathroom sink letting the water run. She ran her fingers over her lips; they were still swollen from kissing Tim for almost two hours at the drive-in. And their bright red hue must have been an announcement to her mother that she hadn't been at the baseball game.

The ice-cold water was a relief. She splashed her hot face again and again, trying to numb the memory of the dream. Her life had become a house of cards, and one wrong move was going to collapse the fragile structure. *If I don't tell Tim—and Mom and Dad—the truth, I'm going to lose everything. I'll do it. Soon.*

Eight

Wednesday afternoon Meg wrote her mother a note: *Went to see Caroline's new house. Be back after dinner. Love—* She checked the directions Caroline had given her over the phone and hopped on her bike.

School had been a groggy haze of doing math worksheets and waiting for bells to ring. At lunch Gretchen had wondered aloud when Billy would make good on his offer to give her driving lessons. Jane and Maria had asked politely about her progress with Tim. Finally Meg had fibbed to the school secretary that she'd just remembered a three o'clock dentist appointment. The thought of last-period French class had been more than she could bear.

As Meg pedaled her bicycle quickly away from her house, the iron grip around her brain loosened. Seeing Caroline always made her feel better.

A glowing, well-tanned version of Caroline

opened the front door. "Meg!" she yelled. "I can't wait to show you the house."

Hugs and kisses out of the way, Caroline ushered Meg around the little house. Hardwood floors gleamed against the carefully placed rag rugs that Caroline's sorority sisters had given her. Meg recognized a soft leather couch from her uncle's downtown office, and Caroline and Rick had given each other an antique four-poster bed as a wedding gift.

"It's adorable," Meg said.

"Thanks." Caroline grinned. "Did you see we gave your collage the place of honor?"

Meg's wedding present hung above their fireplace. "It looks great!" Meg enthused. "I was worried it might end up on the wall of the kitchen pantry or something."

"No way. That's the best present we got!"

"So how was the honeymoon?"

"Absolutely wonderful. I have to admit, it's kind of hard getting back to reality. Everyday life can be pretty mundane."

"I guess." Since Meg had met Tim, her days had been anything but mundane.

"Let's sit down." Caroline moved over to the leather sofa. "I told Rick to make himself scarce so we could talk."

Meg kicked off her shoes and tucked her legs beneath her. "Tell me everything," she said.

Caroline looked at her intently for a moment. "How about *you* tell *me* everything?"

"What do you mean?" There was still a one percent chance that Caroline was referring to something other than Tim.

"I may be married, but I'm still in tune with the grapevine." She paused. "Gloria told me she saw you at the university library with Tim Wilson. She said you guys looked pretty cozy."

"So?"

"So, she filled me in on the wedding reception. About how you told Tim you were a freshman at Vermillion."

"I didn't *tell* him that. He just assumed. . . . Anyway, Gloria was there. She was encouraging me!"

"I know. But she never thought you two would actually start dating. She says she feels like she's guilty of contributing to the delinquency of a minor."

"Give me a break!"

Caroline reached over and ruffled Meg's hair. "Calm down. I'm just kidding." She looked right into Meg's eyes. "She is worried, though—and so am I."

"Is anyone else I should know about worried?"

"Rick."

"Rick! How does he know about Tim and me?"

"He is my *husband,* little cousin. Besides, he ran into Tim on campus this morning."

"What?" Suddenly Meg was sure she'd never hear from Tim again. She'd graduate from high school already an old maid, pining over a man she could never have.

"Relax. He didn't let on about your age. But you put him in a pretty awkward position."

"Jeez. I'm really sorry." This was bad. People all over town knew she was lying. It almost made it worse that they were actually being nice about it.

"We're all just worried that you're in over your

head, Meg." *In over your head.* How many times had she heard that expression in the last few weeks? She wasn't a toddler in the deep end of a swimming pool—she was a woman in love. Or at least a girl in love.

"And lying to Tim isn't really fair," Caroline continued.

"I don't want to lose him," Meg whispered. The pent-up anxiety was becoming overwhelming. She blinked rapidly, trying to force back her tears. It was no use. Tears running down her face, Meg buried her head in her hands. "Great," she said. "Now I'm crying like a baby."

"You're allowed to cry—you're in a tough spot. So why don't you tell me exactly what's been going on? I'll bet you a frozen yogurt that you'll feel better afterward."

Meg brushed away her tears. Wasn't that why she'd gone to Caroline's in the first place? Deep down, she'd been hoping for an opportunity to tell her cousin the whole story. "Well, the night of your wedding, people kept telling me how grown-up I looked. And everything was so romantic. . . ."

Caroline nodded. "Weddings have a tendency to rub off. I think they remind everybody how in love with love they are."

"Exactly. I just felt so perfect, like I was part of a storybook. And Tim was there, and he was so gorgeous. When he thought I was a college girl, I couldn't believe it. I didn't think—"

"Let me guess," Caroline interrupted. "You didn't think it would hurt anybody if you played a little game with him?"

"Yeah. I just wanted to have a great time, and have something to tell Gretchen about. I didn't realize that when the game was over, Tim and I would fall in love."

Caroline looked straight into her eyes. "Are you in love? Really?"

A dull ache spread through Meg's body. She nodded. "I'm really in love. And I think Tim is, too."

Caroline patted Meg's back. "If you're really in love, things will work out. Maybe not the way you think you want them to, though."

"Really?"

"Really. But you've got to come clean with Tim. Secrets like this have a tendency to get out fast."

"How about if I tell him after my birthday? Sixteen sounds a lot better than fifteen."

"Your birthday is over a week away!"

"Please?"

"I'm not going to give you an ultimatum. You have to decide for yourself what you're going to do. As your cousin and your friend, though, I'm warning you. The longer you wait, the more disastrous it's going to be."

Gretchen sat on her bed, a heap of skirts, blouses, and dresses piling up around her. Meg stood in front of her best friend's full-length mirror, wearing sheer pantyhose and a lace bra.

"I don't know what to wear," Meg groaned. "Dressy? Casual? Casually dressy?" Meg rummaged through Gretchen's closet. "Maybe I should borrow something."

"You can borrow whatever you want, but it's all going to be four inches too short," Gretchen answered. "Why don't you wear whatever you feel most comfortable in?"

"What do you think of the black miniskirt and green silk tank top?" Meg asked, holding the top up in front of her.

"Looks great," Gretchen answered.

"No, this shade washes me out," Megan decided, discarding the top.

"How about the black mini and red crop top? It's sexy and sophisticated, but not too dressy. It'll look like you just threw it on at the last minute."

"Perfect. Once again you've saved the day."

"Somehow I don't think picking out an outfit qualifies me for sainthood."

"Combined with the fact that you're letting me sleep over tonight, and covering for me with your parents—that makes you a regular Joan of Arc."

Meg slipped on a pair of black sandals. Exactly four weeks earlier she'd talked to Tim for the first time. Now she couldn't imagine her life without him. Would they make it to their one-year anniversary? Five years?

"Why are you so uptight tonight, anyway? Are you always like this before you see Wonder Boy?"

"I'm always nervous, but tonight's especially important. We're going to Nabil's for dinner."

"Wow. Ritzy."

"How do I look?" Meg did a slow turn in front of Gretchen.

"Beautiful. And not a day under twenty-five."

Meg had swept her hair up on top of her head in

the same style she'd worn the night of Caroline's wedding. Dangling from her ears were the big silver hoops that she'd gotten from her grandmother for her fifteenth birthday. Her only other jewelry was a silver and onyx ring.

"You're sure your parents aren't going to be home until late?" Meg asked.

"Positive. They went to see their old college friends. It's at least a two-hour drive, and they didn't even leave until seven."

"Okay. I'd better take off."

Gretchen walked her down to the front door. "So what are you going to do?" Meg asked.

"Baby-sit. Like I've been doing almost every Saturday night since you met Tim." Gretchen made a face. "Joseph's been playing over at his day-care friend Tony's, but Tony's mom is going to drop him off back home any minute."

"Well, try to have fun."

"Eating mac 'n' cheese and watching taped reruns of *The Flintstones* is always a blast," Gretchen said wryly. "But enough about my pathetic social life. Have a wonderful time being wined and dined by The One."

"Thanks. I'll try."

Meg headed in the direction of Vermillion at a fast pace. The night before her would be perfect. So why did she have the feeling that she should have asked Gretchen to wish her luck?

"Two for Wilson," Tim told the maître d' at Nabil's.

Meg loved Tim's firm hand on her back as they followed the maître d' to their table. The restaurant was bathed in candlelight, and a piano player in the corner provided a background of soft jazz melodies. A single red rose in a vase had been placed at the center of their small table.

"How come no one else has roses?" she asked.

"Because no one else called ahead and told the maître d' that it was their one-month anniversary." He reached across the table and clasped her hand.

"Thank you," she said softly. The pulse at Tim's wrist beat rapidly under her thumb.

"Meg, before I met you, my opinion of women was at a low point. I haven't told you this, but—"

Tim's words were cut off by the approaching waiter. The lettering on the gold-bordered black menus was done in an elegant calligraphy. With the exception of the slow-boiled oxtails, every item Nabil's offered made Meg's mouth water.

Meg glanced up at Tim. "What were you going to say before?" she asked.

As usual, Tim's intense gaze gave her goose-bumps. He opened his mouth, then shut it abruptly.

"Nothing," he finally said. "I just want you to know how much you mean to me."

Tell him now! A voice in Meg's head was screaming at her to confess right there, before they'd even been served their drinks. Tim's expression was so tender, how could he reject her? Maybe they'd end up laughing about Meg's antics by dessert. Then she could think about breaking the news to her parents.

Just say it, she willed herself. "Tim, I have to tell you something. . . ."

"What?"

"I keep meaning to bring it up, but the time never seems right." She was going to do it. The words were already formulated, ready to spill from her tongue out into the romantic atmosphere of the restaurant.

"Just tell me. What is it?"

"That night at Caroline's—" Out of nowhere, the waiter reappeared with a basket of bread. Meg's words died on her lips.

When he was gone, Tim smiled mysteriously. "I think I know what you were going to say just now."

"You do?"

"Yeah. You were going to tell me that you fell in love with me that first night at Caroline's. Maybe it was even love at first sight?"

Meg nodded mutely. "That's it." She managed a smile. "I'll have to add mind reading to the list of your talents."

She'd failed. The throbbing that had started at the back of her head was working its way forward. That was it. She'd had her chance, and she'd blown it.

Tim let out a huge breath. "I felt the same way," he said. "When you were dancing with your father that night, I was standing at the edge of the terrace, staring at you. I had this crazy fantasy that it was *our* wedding. I imagined how we would run upstairs and grab our suitcases—how we'd sneak out, just the two of us. Almost like we were doing something wrong."

I am doing something wrong, she wanted to shout. Tim had a sheepish grin on his face; it was as if all the sunlight from the days of the past month had been stored behind his eyes. He was no longer the fantasy guy whom she'd worshiped for months from afar.

He was more. He was a real person. The wisdom of Gretchen's and Caroline's warnings came crashing down around her. Tim wouldn't just be angry if he found out she'd been lying to him. He wouldn't just tell her to get lost and then ride off into the sunset. His hurt would be as profound as her own. *I've betrayed him,* she thought. *Before he even knew me, I betrayed him.*

But Tim didn't really know her now, did he? She let him think he did. She told him vague stories about classes and friends and college activities. She'd made Gretchen into her pretend roommate at Carman Hall. She even mentioned her parents in passing. But all of those details were varying degrees of one massive lie. The lie of her life.

On the outside, Meg was chatting with Tim. She was holding his hand, smiling, playing footsie. She ate the prawns she'd ordered and said how delicious they were. She tried a bite of Tim's filet mignon, sipped her mineral water, nibbled at a piece of bread.

On the inside, she argued with herself. It wasn't just Tim she was hurting. Her obsession with Tim and the double life she'd been leading were causing her to neglect Gretchen. She never asked Gretch how *she* was doing anymore; she either complained about feeling guilty or stared off into space, preoccupied. Like that night. She'd spent time with Gretchen only in order to spend more time with Tim.

And the way she'd been treating her parents . . . she'd effectively shut them out of her life. When they thought she was at the library with Gretchen, she was at a movie with Tim. When they were waiting for her to be dropped off by Mr. Rubin after a party, she was running through the dark streets, thinking up new lies to tell them.

After the waiter had cleared their plates, Tim pulled a small box out of his jacket pocket.

"What's that?" she asked.

"I wanted to give you something. Sort of an old-fashioned token that we're officially going steady."

The box was pale blue, its only wrapping an ivory silk bow. Meg handled the box gently; it felt almost alive at the touch of her fingertips.

"Oh, Tim. You didn't have to give me anything."

"But I wanted to. Open it."

Inside was a simple silver heart attached to a delicate matching chain. The flat silver pendant shone against her palm.

"It's beautiful," she breathed.

"Turn it over."

"'M.—Love always—T.,'" she read aloud. "Tim, I don't know what to say."

"Say you'll wear it."

"I will. Of course I'll wear it." She was a fraud. No better than a con artist.

"Good. Now what should we order for dessert?"

As Meg picked up her dessert menu her eyes scanned Nabil's dim interior. Most of the tables were occupied by older couples. The easy way they laughed and debated was enviable. Her eyes were drawn back to a couple at the other side of the room.

She gasped inwardly. *It's the Johnsons!* Her next-door neighbors and her parents' occasional bridge partners were calmly eating their salads. What if they'd seen her? She had to get out of there. Fast. For the hundredth time that night, she cursed herself.

"Tim, do you mind if we skip dessert?"

"Now you're talking. Let's go somewhere to be alone."

"No, I . . . I have this horrible headache. I didn't want to ruin our night, but it's gotten worse all of a sudden." The sight of Tim's disappointed face was almost too much to bear. "Could you take me back to the dorm?"

"Sure. If that's what you want."

"I'm sorry."

"Why don't you wait in the car?" he said stiffly. "I'll be out in a minute."

Meg kept her head down as she passed the Johnsons' table. She race-walked the rest of the way out and climbed quickly into Tim's car. Her head really was pounding. She massaged her temples, thinking. How could she make this up to Tim? There had to be a way.

They drove to Vermillion in awkward silence. Tim came around and opened her door. Instead of the usual lingering kisses, he pecked her cheek and gave her shoulder a quick squeeze. "Feel better."

"Thanks. Listen, I love the necklace. You're wonderful."

"Sure. You're welcome."

"I mean it."

"Why don't you give me a call? I'll be waiting."

"Sweet dreams," she whispered as he vanished back into the dark car. "I love you." *Only someone in love could feel as miserable as I feel right now,* she added silently.

Nine

Tears streamed down Meg's face as her sandals clapped rhythmically against the pavement. Streetlights cast huge, wavy shadows of her moving figure. Her lungs felt as if they would burst; gasping for air, she finally slowed to a walk when she neared Macon Street, two blocks from Gretchen's.

What had she been running from? Herself? Tim? In a way, she'd been running for the past month, running all out to get away from the restrictions of her young age. But why was it so wrong to want to experience the world now? She'd been tired of going through the motions of high school, fed up with hoping a guy whose biggest accomplishment was catching the winning football pass would ask her to the stupid prom. Tim made her think. He made her feel.

Meg stopped when she saw the green Fiat parked in front of Gretchen's house. Billy Jenkins. It shouldn't have been such a shock. Billy had as much as asked Gretchen out that night at the mall. But Gretchen hadn't mentioned him since. Or had she? Again, Meg realized how little attention she'd been paying to other people's lives lately.

"Meg, what're you doing standing in the street? Come inside!" Gretchen's bright voice came from behind her front screen door.

"Yeah, I'm coming," Meg called back. She trudged up the brick path.

"Why are you back so early?" Gretchen asked. She peered through the darkness at Meg's tear-stained face. "You've been crying," she said more softly. "What happened?"

"I don't want to talk about it right now. You didn't say *he* was going to be here." She motioned toward Billy's convertible with her head.

"I didn't know. He just stopped by, and he's been here for two *hours*," Gretchen whispered.

"I don't want to interrupt your good time."

"Don't be an idiot. We're just playing Go Fish with Joseph."

"Billy's playing with Joey? He doesn't seem the type." Billy "Motorcycle Boots" Jenkins was helping Gretchen baby-sit? *The whole town must be in the twilight zone*, Meg thought.

"I *know*. But the little brat loves him! You've got to see it to believe it. Come on."

"Wait. Who's the little brat, Billy or Joseph?"

"Ha, ha. Just come into the den."

"Hey there, Meg," Billy greeted her. The heartthrob of Southwest High was sitting across from Gretchen's six-year-old brother at a miniature card table.

"Hi, Billy. Hi, Joey."

"Hi, Meg," Joey answered.

"Sevens," Billy said.

"Go fish." Joseph looked up at Meg. "Gretch says I'm not supposed to tell Mom you weren't helping her baby-sit."

"Your sister has a big mouth. But she's right." Meg glowered at Gretchen.

"I had to," Gretchen murmured back.

"Good luck with the game, guys. I'm gonna go up to bed."

Gretchen followed her to the stairs. "I'll be up pretty soon," she said. "We can talk."

"Don't make Billy leave on my account. At least one of us should have a good time tonight."

"Well, I have to get Joey ready for bed in a few minutes. We'll see what happens."

"Hey, Gretch?"

"Yeah?"

"Billy seems really nice. You know, now that he's not just some junior we talk about on the phone."

"He is nice." Gretchen gave her a little wave and trotted back into the den.

Meg walked heavily up the stairs. From the other room, she heard the distinct chime of Gretchen's giggles.

"Meg, are you awake?" Gretchen whispered in the general direction of Meg's twin bed.

"Yeah." Her voice sounded unnaturally loud in the quiet room.

Gretchen switched on a small lamp on her

dresser and searched for a clean nightgown. "You want to tell me why you were crying earlier? Did Tim find out?"

"In answer to the first question: maybe in a little bit. Second question: no, but I almost wish he had. That ties into why I was crying."

Gretchen pulled on a nightshirt that said Southwest Is Never Far Behind on the back. "I really think it would help if you talked about it."

"Tell me what's going on with Billy first."

"Are you sure you're in the mood?" Gretchen switched off the light and climbed into bed.

"Sure I'm sure. Now tell me what you've been doing downstairs for the last—" She leaned over and glanced at a digital clock glowing on the nightstand. "—hour and forty-five minutes!"

"Well, I put Joey to bed. That took a while—he was ultra hyper. I think we let him eat too much chocolate while we were playing cards—"

"How about skipping to the good part? Did he kiss you?"

"Yes! Right before he left. And he said he'd call me!" Gretchen hugged her pillow close to her body. "Meg, it was like a dream. I've never felt so . . . so . . . ."

"Weightless?"

"Yeah. I mean, I feel like that now. A hurricane could hit the house and I'd be outside dancing. But—"

"But what?"

"When it was actually happening—or right before—I was so nervous, I thought I was going to burst into hysterical laughter. I was sure I had bad breath, or our teeth were going to clink together and make some really awful sound."

"None of that happened, though. Right?"

"Right." Gretchen sighed. "I haven't even told you the best part."

"Don't keep me in suspense," Meg prompted.

"He asked me to the junior prom."

"He did? Wow."

"Yeah. He told me that Jared Colburn's going to ask Maria tomorrow. If she says yes—which she will—we're going to double with them."

"That's great, Gretch. I'm really happy for you."

"Thanks." She was quiet for a moment. "Hey, Meg?"

"What?"

"You don't mind, do you? About Billy?"

"Why?"

"Well, I know you've got Tim now—I think—but you had a crush on Billy for so long. I never thought . . ."

"It's all right." Meg put her hands behind her head and stared up at the glow-in-the-dark constellation stickers that Gretchen had put on the ceiling. "I admit a part of me *is* a little jealous, but mostly I just feel glad that you've met someone you like. Going to the junior prom would be fun."

"I thought you said high school dances were boring and stupid!"

"They are," Meg sighed. "But they're also kind of fun." She reached up and touched the silver heart that lay in the hollow of her throat. "If you're into that type of thing."

"It's your turn to spill some guts. What're the characters on *The Too Young and Restless* up to?"

"I think this is the climactic moment when we

hear the omniscient narrator—that's you—say, 'I told you so.'"

"That bad, huh?"

"Yes. No. I don't know."

"Expand."

"Tim gave me this necklace tonight." Meg turned on the light and held the heart up for Gretchen to inspect. She flipped it so that Gretchen could read the back.

"Whoa. That's pretty heavy—but I don't get it. Shouldn't you be *happy?*"

"I'd be *ecstatic,* except that part of me feels like Tim gave this necklace to a total stranger. I can't go on like this. I want to be able to tell him everything."

"That's understandable," Gretchen said sympathetically.

"I want to talk to him about school and my parents . . . even the junior prom. As much as I say I hate being in high school, it *is* a pretty significant part of my life."

"Sounds like you've decided to tell him the truth."

"Yep. The day after my birthday, I'm going to drop the bomb—for better or worse, I'm going to do it."

"I've missed you," Tim said.

Meg buried her face against his chest and hugged him tight. "I've missed you, too." Her voice was muffled against his yellow cotton T-shirt.

They hadn't seen each other for a whole week. Their conversation the Sunday after their ill-fated one-month anniversary dinner had been tense, but over the last few days things had almost gone back to normal.

As the days went by Meg checked them off on her mental calendar. *Six days until I have to tell Tim . . . Four days . . . Tomorrow is my birthday—two days.*

Her birthday had been marked by a gold keyring from her parents and a hand-painted silk scarf from Caroline. Gretchen gave her a silver and turquoise bracelet. "Wear it for luck," Gretchen had whispered as Meg's mother brought out the German chocolate cake she baked every year.

That morning Meg had opened her eyes wide at dawn. "Today is the day," she'd announced to no one in particular. In response, the birds outside had seemed to chirp even louder. "I'm glad someone's in a good mood," she'd grumbled.

"Let's not let another seven days go by before we see each other again." Tim's voice brought Meg back to the present. Back to D-Day. *I hope you're still saying that an hour from now,* she thought gloomily.

"So what have you been up to? How's your roommate?"

Tim laughed. "The same as always. He's convinced he's in love with a girl in his Intro to Economics class, but he's not sure how to break the news to her boyfriend on the wrestling team."

"Sounds like blood-and-guts time."

"Yeah. He'll probably just forget about her, though." Tim pulled Meg close. "Ollie's not like me. He takes stuff like relationships pretty lightly."

"Oh." Meg decided Oliver probably wasn't a good topic of conversation. "Do you want to walk over to the swing set?" she asked. "If you're nice, I'll let you push me."

"Promises, promises."

With Tim's arm around her waist, Meg led him down the tree-lined path toward the playground.

"Meg! Wait up."

Meg turned to see Felicia Willis and Alana Sullivan, Jane's ninth-grade sister, heading in her direction.

"Who's that?" Tim asked.

"No one. One of them, Alana, is my friend's little sister." Why did she have to run into them just then? Couldn't they have just waved from a distance and kept walking?

"Hi, guys," Meg greeted the smiling girls.

"Hi, Meg," Alana answered breathlessly. "Gosh, I was worried we'd never catch up to you—we saw you from all the way across the park. I wanted to say happy late birthday."

"Oh . . . thanks." *Why now? Oh, God, why now?*

Tim shot her a look.

"You're so lucky to be sixteen. I have to wait almost two more years! But I'm making Jane teach me to drive as soon as she gets her license. She doesn't want to, but my mom said—"

Meg stared at the whole group in horrified silence. The trees were spinning, and the brick walkway was looming up close. "Tim, I—"

"Meg, you've said—or haven't said—enough. What kind of idiot do you think I am?"

"Let me explain," she begged as Alana and Felicia scurried off.

Tim started walking fast.

"Tim, stop!" Meg yelled.

"What're you going to say, Meg? They have you confused with someone else? You're only *pretending* to be a tenth grader—you're really an undercover cop working on a case? What?" Tim was screaming, his voice echoing on the quiet playground.

"No! I was going to tell you the truth—today. I swear! That's why I wanted to go sit on the swing set . . . to explain."

"Yeah, right. Like you haven't had plenty of chances to tell me before. The night we met, for instance, might have been a good time."

"Calm down. Please. Just for a minute."

"How do you think I felt yesterday, knowing that it was your birthday and that you were celebrating with someone else? Do you have another boyfriend, too? Maybe some cute eleventh grader you pass notes with during study hall?"

"Of course I don't have another boyfriend. And I'm sorry that—" She paused. "Wait a second. How did you know my birthday was yesterday?"

"That girl just said so!"

"She said, 'Happy late birthday.' How do you know my birthday wasn't last week? Or even last month?"

"I don't know. Maybe I'm psychic. Who cares? The point is, you've been lying to me all along. Just like—" Tim stopped.

"Like who?"

"Nobody!"

Why was she trying to argue? Nothing she said was going to change the fact that she'd kept the truth from him. "If you want to hate me, I totally understand."

"Don't be ridiculous. I can't hate you. I still love you."

Meg grabbed his arms and made him face her. She looked into his eyes. "You still love me?" she whispered.

Tim perched on top of a nearby picnic table, his head in his hands. "I don't know what I feel," he said finally.

"Please don't shut me out." She put a tentative hand on his knee.

Tim picked up her hand; he held it for a moment, then gently let it go. "I noticed things," he said, almost to himself. "Little details. Like you never actually came out of Carman when I was picking you up. And you didn't talk about friends much. But it wasn't until . . . Well, it wasn't until lately that I really started putting two and two together. I didn't want to believe it."

"I really messed things up."

"*Life* is messed up. You think you know someone. You love them. You trust them. You dream about being with them forever. And then they stab you in the back, like they never really cared about you at all. Why?"

He wasn't even talking to her. He was looking off into the distance at an invisible audience. It was as if a camera was rolling and he was delivering a last soliloquy before the final fade to black.

The cold tone in his voice was like a door being slammed in her face. "You *can* trust me. I love you. That's why I was scared. . . ."

"Scared to tell me the truth? Scared to let me into your life? I could have dealt with your age— maybe—but you took me for a fool."

"I never thought you were a fool! How can you

say that?" The conversation was an anguished circle of accusations and defenses. It didn't matter that she felt as if she were going to die. No amount of pleading would help her obtain the mercy of the court. Tim was judge and jury.

"How can either of us say anything? Being betrayed isn't like forgetting to call or being late for a date, Meg. It's the destruction of the soul."

The resignation in Tim's voice was terrifying. The air around Meg felt terribly heavy and constricting. She began to feel as if it were suffocating her, threatening to block out her vision and squeeze her heart dry.

"Is this it? Am I never going to see you again?" she asked.

"I don't know. I just don't know." He got up and began walking away. He turned his head to look at her. "Look, I need to be alone right now."

"Call me!" she screamed to his retreating figure.

Tim shook his head and continued down the path.

What should she do? Going home was out of the question. Parents and questions were about as appealing as another cozy chat with Alana and Felicia. Gretchen would be sympathetic, but eventually the conversation would turn to buying a dress for the junior prom. She wasn't exactly up to a shopping spree at the mall.

In a daze, Meg walked over to the bright orange swing set. That was the spot where she'd been planning to tell Tim her secret. Would she have gone through with it? Would how he found out the truth really have made any difference?

Wedged into the small swing, Meg pushed off with her feet. She pumped her legs, swinging higher and higher. She could feel the huge bars of the set shift dangerously under her weight. Instead of slowing down, she threw her body into the forward-and-backward motion of the swing.

Meg's wrenching sobs were drowned out by the rushing wind and the unforgiving creak of the hinges.

Ten

Meg didn't want to leave her room. A minute away from the phone was sixty seconds during which she might miss Tim's call. So she studied. She outlined history chapters, did math problems, practiced reading French out loud. If she could have borrowed the equipment from school, she probably would have set up a science lab in her bedroom. Looming final exams kept her sane.

It had been over a week since Tim had shaken his head and walked away. The college semester was almost over, and he hadn't called. She was about to officially become a junior in high school, get her driver's license, and start her summer job as a day counselor at Sherwood Camp. And he hadn't called. But he would. He had to.

Monday afternoon Gretchen opened the door to Meg's room and picked her way through piles of flash cards and dog-eared notebooks. "Meg, you have to get a grip," she said.

"I *have* a grip," Meg answered defiantly. "I'm acing my exams. I organized my summer clothes. I even gave myself a pedicure." She held out her passion-pink toenails for Gretchen's inspection.

"You have to get a *mental* grip. Your mom's threatening torture if I don't tell her what's wrong with you."

Meg sighed. "My last exam is tomorrow. I'll deal with everything after that, okay?"

"Promise?"

"Yeah. I'll even tell my mom what's been going on for the last six weeks. How mad can she be now that the whole thing is over?"

"With any luck, she'll start spouting psychobabble about a teenager's unconscious need to rebel. Or something."

"With any luck, she won't say anything. She'll just ground me for the rest of my miserable life."

"He's going to call, Meg. You just have to give him some time."

"Right now time is all I have. Lots of endless, empty, lonely, meaningless time."

Meg squinted against the glare of the sun. Her last exam had been over for ten whole minutes, and all she wanted to do was go somewhere and cry. *I should have taken six college prep courses*, she thought. *Then I'd still have something to study for*. The Latin nerds wouldn't be done until Wednesday.

Kids were sprawled all over Southwest's big

lawn. "Hey, Meg," Maria called. "Do you want to sign my yearbook?"

Meg smiled weakly. "Maybe later," she called back. "I, uh, have to get home."

"Whatever you say." Maria whispered something to the girl next to her, who glanced at Meg and nodded solemnly.

Great. By ten o'clock that night the whole school would know that she'd gotten dumped. What an awesome way to kick off the summer.

She saw him first out of the corner of her eye. He was leaning against his car in the parking lot, wearing khaki shorts and a university track team T-shirt. Before her mind could fully register that it was Tim, Meg's heart began to race and hot blood started to pound in her ears.

In less than thirty seconds, she was standing before him.

"Hi," he said simply. "All done with finals?"

"Yeah. You?"

"I finished last night."

"That's great. I'm sure you did really well."

"Yeah . . . whatever. It was kind of hard to care." Meg nodded.

"I think we should talk." His tone was eerily formal.

"Here?"

"Nah. Let's go somewhere."

"Where?"

"How about—" He looked around. "The bleachers by the football field. For once, we'll be on *your* turf." His attempt at a smile didn't quite reach his eyes.

"Sure. Sounds good." Should she hope? Had he come to make up, or was this a last good-bye?

Without a screaming coach and guys running around in pads and helmets, the football field was eerily empty. They sat at the very top of the bleachers. When Meg looked down, she could see the trash that had fallen through the bleachers' metal slats.

"So," Tim said.

"Do you forgive me?" Meg couldn't hold back the question any longer.

"In a way, yes. As hard as I've tried, I can't stay mad at you. I wanted to. Believe me, I wanted to. But instead of being angry, I just feel lousy."

"Me too." Every emotion she'd ever experienced coursed through her veins. She was breathless.

"I still love you."

"Oh, Tim. I love you too. I'm so sorry all of this happened. Can we start over? I won't keep any more secrets. I swear."

Tim sighed. He ran his fingers through his hair, leaving the top sticking straight up. "I wish it were that easy. I wish I could just laugh it off and take you in my arms and kiss you." His gaze fell on her trembling lips.

"But?"

"But I can't. Jeez, Meg. You're barely sixteen. I'm not even sure going out with you is *legal*, much less ethical."

"That's stupid. If I were twenty-one and you were twenty-four, no one would even raise an eyebrow."

"But you're not twenty-one."

"I will be someday."

Tim laughed. "Man, I've missed you. It's almost

scary how much I've been wanting to talk to you every day."

"I feel the same way! Tim, I'll make my parents understand. I won't lie to them about us anymore. I was going to tell them anyway—"

"Meg, stop. It's not that simple. Your age is part of what's between us, but it's not all."

"What else?"

"I just can't trust you right now. I need some time to sort things out."

"What does that mean? What are you going to do?"

"Remember how I told you I applied for an internship with Senator Higgins in Washington, D.C.?"

"Yeah. But that was so long ago. You never heard from them. You said you'd decided to stay here and take classes and—"

"I heard. After that day in the park. I got back to the dorm, and the letter was waiting—I got the internship."

Meg felt sick to her stomach. She gripped the bleacher seat and closed her eyes. "You're going."

"That letter was like a sign. I have to get away from here for a while. I have to escape."

"So I won't see you?"

"No."

"But you'll be back in the fall, right? It's not like we're never going to see each other again."

"I don't know. I'm thinking about trying to transfer to Georgetown." He shifted his weight, keeping his eyes turned resolutely away from hers.

"So this is it. This is the end. Good-bye, Meg and Tim—"

"Stop! I can't stand this. Nothing's written in stone. Maybe someday, when you're older and this is all behind us . . ."

"Sure." Meg's voice broke. "Someday."

Their last kiss was bittersweet. Tim held her tightly for a long time before he pushed her gently away from him. "Give me a few minutes to get to my car and drive away," he whispered.

Meg nodded, pressing her lips together tightly. Tim ran lightly down the bleachers, his muscles sleek in the sunlight. He didn't look back.

The chiffon dress was midnight blue. It swished against the floor as Meg pattered from her dressing table to the full-length mirror. "I guess this is what they call getting back into the swing of things," she told her reflection.

It had taken Gretchen six days to convince Meg to go to the junior prom with Billy's friend, Peter Lang. "He doesn't have to be your dream man," Gretchen had said. "Just have a good time with him. No one's expecting you to fall in love."

"What about your double date with Maria?" Meg had reminded her.

"Please, Meg—Maria knows that you're my best friend," Gretchen had answered. "Anyway, she'd rather double date with Jane."

Except for Meg, the decision that she should go on a blind date to the prom had been unanimous. Gretchen, Caroline, and even her newly informed mother had ganged up against her. "Meg, I'm *making* you go," Mrs. Henry had said. "If you mope around the house any longer, I might lose my mind. Now get in the car. We're going to get you a dress."

That had been the end of the discussion. She had gotten the dress, the shoes, the jewelry. Her mom had picked up a boutonniere at the florist that morning. In minutes, her date would be ringing the doorbell.

In spite of her sadness, she couldn't help smiling when she slipped on her new pumps. High heels always made her feel elegant. *I hope this guy is at least over five foot eight,* she thought.

The skirt of her dress swirled around her as she spun in front of the mirror. Her hair was tied back with a white silk ribbon, and she had a matching shawl to throw over her shoulders.

I've changed, she realized. The face in the mirror was calm and self-confident. The night of her makeover and first dance with Tim seemed a lifetime ago. She was really a woman now.

And women didn't laze around and sulk. They went after the moment, seized the day. If being with Tim had taught her anything, it was the importance of being herself and cherishing every second of happiness that crossed her path. *Because I'd do it all again,* she thought. *I'd do it differently, but I'd do it again.*

Those weeks with Tim had been worth the ache she now felt in her heart. But if she couldn't be with him, she might as well enjoy the things that she'd sacrificed during their time together. Friends. High school. Her relationship with her parents. Without Tim, those elements of her life were more important than ever.

Downstairs, the doorbell chimed. *Show time,* she thought, picking up her new deep blue evening bag and taking one last look in the mirror. *Peter Lang's not going to know what hit him.*

Standing nervously at the front door, Peter's smile seemed to light up his face. In his rented tux, he didn't make Meg's heart race the way that Tim had the night Caroline got married. But he didn't look half bad. Amid her mother's fussing and the flash of her father's camera, Peter's hands trembled slightly as he pinned on the white orchid corsage he'd brought.

"It's lovely," Meg said, and smiled. She pinned on Peter's single red rose boutonniere without a trace of the jitters. Attitude, she'd learned, was everything.

Billy and Gretchen were waiting in Peter's car. "Gretchen didn't want her hair to get messed up in the Fiat," Peter explained as they walked away from Meg's house.

"It'll be fun to go together," Meg answered, waving at Gretchen.

As they pulled away from the curb Gretchen leaned forward and whispered in Meg's ear. "How's it going? I think he's kind of cute."

"Fine, I think," Meg whispered back. "I'm managing to make small talk *and* smile."

"You've come a long way, baby."

Yeah, Meg thought. *I really have.* The image of Tim's face, with his curly lashes and sexy smile, swam before her face. A pang of longing pierced her heart. She still had a long way to go.

•   •   •

Cool wind whipped through Meg's hair as she drove down the freeway outside of town. It was impossible to believe that only two weeks earlier she hadn't had her license. The mere thought of being confined to walking or riding her bike made her feel like a dog on a leash. *This is what I've needed,* she reflected. *The ability to go out on my own and explore uncharted territory.* She had to be home by eleven o'clock, but in the meantime she could drive for hours in any direction—no questions asked. If only she could share her sense of freedom with Tim, life would truly be perfect.

I wonder how long it would take me to get to Washington, D.C.? It was only a few hundred miles away. She could get there in a few hours. Meg turned up the radio and pressed her foot down harder on the gas pedal. Allowing her mind to drift, she pictured their reunion. She could almost feel Tim in her arms. Meg saw herself showing up at the front door of his cozy brownstone just as the sun was setting . . . he would look deep into her eyes and pull her to him without a word. Their kiss would burn her lips, sending a tingling sensation spreading all through her body.

She blinked her eyes, and a tear slid down her cheek. She'd been trying not to think about how much she missed Tim. But just the day before she'd started to cry when she'd driven past the 64th Street drive-in movie theater. And the week before she'd jogged through the university campus, looking at each building. She'd studied each doorway, imagining Tim walking through it with his backpack over one shoulder. Now he might never walk across campus again. She might not even be able to hide behind the bleachers and watch him play soccer in the fall. He might wind up living in D.C., maybe even dating somebody else. . . .

Meg missed her exit off the highway. *I'm seriously in space!* she realized, trying to shake the picture of Tim out of her mind. If only she could know what he was doing. Was he happy? Did he like his internship? Had he applied to Georgetown? Unanswered questions raced through her mind, and she let the tears flow freely. On the highway, there was no one to see her cry, no one to tell her to grow up and move on. If only she could make people realize that moving on was impossible. She couldn't just fall out of love. . . .

She forced her thoughts away from her desire to be with Tim. *Get it together, Meg. There's absolutely no way that you can go see Tim.* She smiled wistfully and blew him an imaginary kiss good-bye.

Meg switched on the cruise control and leaned back in the plush seat of her father's car. *On the other hand,* she thought, *a little fantasizing never hurt anybody. After all, a girl can dare to dream. . . .*

Part II
HE SAID

Eleven

"You're a lucky man, Wilson."

"Why's that?" Tim Wilson asked his roommate, Oliver Staley.

"Rumor has it the best-looking women on campus are going to be at Caroline Henry's wedding." Oliver sat on his side of the messy room, bouncing a basketball against the wall. The incessant thumping was distracting Tim from a pressing matter—how to get his black bow tie straight.

"Caroline didn't invite me. Rick did." Tim groaned in frustration as the bow tie fell apart in his hands. His expression was pained as he craned his neck and started from scratch. "Do girls have this much trouble getting into pantyhose?" he wondered aloud.

"More. Imagine if your bow tie could get a run. You'd be on your fifth one by now."

"Thanks for the encouragement. Think you could do any better?"

"As a matter of fact, yes," Oliver said, crossing the room. He grabbed the two ends of Tim's tie and crossed the material under and over. "I've had a few occasions to wear a tux."

"Well, I haven't. This thing is going to strangle me!"

"Just remember the girls, my man. They go wild for a guy in a monkey suit." Oliver stood back and surveyed his perfect bow.

"Don't even mention girls to me. I'm on permanent hiatus from the female species."

"Come on, Tim. This is your chance to bounce back from that heinous creature you called a girlfriend."

"Her name is Melinda."

"Melinda, schmelinda. You need a new attitude and a hot date."

"Maybe." Tim sighed. Why did Ollie have to bring up Melinda? Even saying her name in passing made him feel as if a heavyweight boxer had punched him in the gut.

"Did I hear you say maybe? Call the reporters—I think you're making actual progress!"

"Look, I'd be happy to go on a date . . . if there were anyone worth asking."

"Tim, this university is filled with babes. Not only are they coming out of the woodwork, but last semester they were spilling onto the soccer field— to see you, freshman superstar, make goals."

"That was last semester," Tim said. "A lot of things were different then," he added heavily.

"What was so different? In the fall you were mooning around campus because the girl of your dreams was hundreds of miles away. Now it's spring, and you're still down in the dumps."

"Correction. Now I've been dumped by the girl of my dreams."

"Dude, she did you a favor. Now you can take advantage of your jock status and go out with some awesome-looking girls." Oliver began rummaging through his laundry bag.

"Don't you get it? I'm not interested in dating some girl who's attracted to me because I'm good at soccer or run a five-minute mile. I need a woman like—"

"Like that shrew who cheated on you the second your back was turned?"

"I just don't want to go out with someone who likes me for superficial reasons."

"Hey, if you want to waste the four best years of your life sulking in this room because your high school sweetheart turned out to be a dud, that's your business."

"Damn right it is."

"Will you do me one favor?" Oliver had pulled a semi-wrinkled shirt from his massive pile of dirty laundry. He was buttoning it up as he slid his feet into a pair of worn-out loafers.

"What?"

"At least *look* at the girls tonight."

Tim laughed. "Do you ever give up?"

"I'll give up when I'm old and gray, stuck in some retirement home."

"You win. I'll look." *But it's not going to do any good,* he added silently.

"And if you actually open your eyes, you might even see something you like."

"I wouldn't lay odds on it," Tim said glumly.

Oliver put one hand on the doorknob. "Man, in this life you can't lay odds on anything." The door banged shut behind him.

Tim sat down on his own neatly made twin bed. He opened the small drawer of his college-issue bedside table. The glossy senior photo of his ex-girlfriend, Melinda Warren, was exactly where he'd left it that morning, the corner of its gold frame sticking out from under a pile of last semester's Introduction to Eastern Religion notes. *Buried treasure,* Tim thought, picking up the photo.

He'd been trying to shut her out of his mind for weeks. It was no use. How could he say good-bye to the girl he'd thought he'd be with forever? The picture in his hand seemed to breathe as he ran his fingertips over the image of Melinda's thick auburn curls and cool green eyes. The first time they'd kissed, her red lips had trembled beneath his. Now those lips were kissing some guy named George.

George. He'd sounded harmless enough when Melinda mentioned him during a phone conversation in January. "He's a good guy to know," she'd said. "George is in advanced calculus. You know what a ditz I am when it comes to math." Tim let out a bitter laugh. George was probably not only helping with her math homework, but taking her tests for her as well.

Melinda's smiling face blurred in front of Tim's eyes. He lay back on his bed, the frame propped on his chest. When he closed his eyes, that horrible night came rushing back.

There had been snow everywhere. It was February fourteenth, and Tim had been miserable thinking about Melinda being so far away on Valentine's Day. In the middle of a conversation with Oliver, Tim had grabbed an overnight bag and picked up his car keys. "I can't take it anymore," he'd announced. "I need to see Melinda—tonight."

"Wilson, have you lost your mind? Another blizzard's supposed to hit tonight."

"Who cares? In seven hours, I'll be up the coast and nestled in Melinda's dorm room. That's what I call a Valentine's Day."

"Not if you're stranded on some deserted highway."

"Chill out, Ollie. I've got snow tires."

"At least call her and let her know you're on your way. If you don't show up, she can send out the National Guard."

"And ruin the surprise? No way."

Oliver had shaken his head. "Love does crazy things to people," he'd said.

Nine hours later, Tim had pulled up in front of Melinda's dormitory. As Oliver had predicted, snow had started to fall at twilight. Two hours from the small college town, the driver's side windshield wiper on Tim's car had given out. After nearly a hundred miles of leaning out the car to wipe the windshield by hand, Tim had been convinced that his fingers were going to fall off from frostbite. *But it's worth it,* he'd thought. In just minutes, those numb fingers would stroke the ivory skin of Melinda's face.

Tim had dug the long-stemmed chocolate roses he'd gotten from the local 7-Eleven out of the back seat of his Oldsmobile. He'd brushed through his shaggy blond hair with his fingers and taken a deep breath. In spite of the freezing cold, his heart had been beating fast and drops of sweat had been running down his face. *Maybe I should have called,* he'd thought nervously. *Mel could be in the library, or at a friend's, or . . .* He had been half tempted to drive back to the 7-Eleven and use the pay phone.

Instead he'd stridden up the path that led to Melinda's dorm and knocked firmly on the heavy wooden door. When there was no sound from within, he had tentatively tried to push it open. The knob had turned easily in his hand, and a rush of warm air enveloped his face. *This is it,* he'd thought. *She's probably right upstairs.*

Tim had taken the stairs two at a time. On the third floor he'd taken a right and gone to the end of the long hall. Every door he passed had a construction paper cutout with the resident's name written on it. In front of a bright red paper balloon that said *Melinda Warren* in a large, sprawling cursive, he'd stopped. Melinda's soft giggles floated through the door and into the hallway.

He'd tucked the candy flowers behind his back and rapped lightly on the door with his knuckles.

"Who is it?"

Tim had swallowed hard. He couldn't believe that she was only inches away. "It's your crazy boyfriend, who missed you so much he drove hundreds of miles in the—"

The door had flown open. "Tim! What are you doing here?" Melinda's auburn hair hung loosely around her face. Her cheeks were flushed a rosy pink. Tim's gaze had traveled from her bare feet to her wide green eyes.

"Happy Valentine's Day!" He'd held out the foil-covered flowers and opened his arms wide.

Melinda had moved to block the doorway. "You should have called," she'd said. She had looked over her shoulder into the room and jerked her head.

"I wanted to surprise you. Now, are you going to kiss me? My lips feel like ice cubes." The look of shock on her face had been award-winning.

"Tim, I—"

"Who's there, Mel?" a deep voice had said from the back of Melinda's small room.

Tim's heart had stopped. "Her *boyfriend*," he'd yelled, taking a step past Melinda.

A tall, dark-haired guy had been lounging comfortably on Melinda's bed. He'd been holding against his chest the teddy bear Tim had won for her at a carnival the previous summer. The guy had flung the stuffed animal aside and stood up. "What—? Melinda, what's going on?"

"What are *you* doing sitting on my girlfriend's bed?" Tim had shouted. He'd turned to Melinda. "Who is this guy?"

Melinda had been looking back and forth without saying a word. Tucking her loose white silk shirt into the waistband of her black miniskirt, she'd bit her lip. "Tim, meet George." She had glanced across the room. "George, meet Tim."

"This is George? The guy you've been getting to help you in calculus?" Tim had taken in Melinda's appearance with fresh eyes. The way her hair was falling out of its barrette. The pink in her cheeks. The untucked shirt. "Oh, no."

George had laughed. "Helping her with homework? Is that what she told you? Beautiful."

Tim had been clenching his jaw muscles so tightly they ached. He'd dropped the chocolate roses on Melinda's desk. The roar in his ears had been deafening. "Tell him to get out of here," Tim had said quietly. "Now."

Melinda had shifted from one foot to the other. "George, do you mind? I need to talk to Tim for a while. I'll call you later."

George had raised his eyebrows and stared at Tim. "Sure. But you'd better come up with a good excuse about why Wonder Dog here doesn't know about us yet."

"George, please. I'll talk to you later."

George had shrugged. "So long, Tim. Too bad I won't be seeing you around." The door had slammed shut behind him.

Melinda had picked up the teddy bear that George had left half dangling over the side of the bed and sat down. "I don't know what to say—"

"Shut up," Tim had interrupted. "Just shut up."

"Don't be an idiot. We need to talk." She'd patted the spot next to her.

Tim had shuddered. He'd yanked Melinda's chair out from behind her desk and sunk down onto it. Only one word had come to mind: *Why?*

"Is this it? Are you actually dating that Neanderthal?"

The words had practically choked him.

"Tim, I'm sorry. Really. I've been meaning to tell you, but . . ."

"But what? It just slipped your mind while you

were making kissing noises over the phone and telling me you loved me?"

"I didn't want to hurt you."

"Yeah, right. That's why you were making out with your math tutor while I was driving halfway up the East Coast in a blizzard."

"You're not making this easy."

"What do you want me to do? Give you away at the wedding?"

"Don't you understand?" Melinda had shouted. "You're hundreds of miles away! I've been lonely."

"What about me? Don't you think I'm lonely?"

"Yes," she had whispered.

"What about the promises we made? What about being in love?"

"Things change, Tim. If you were here, it might be another story. But you're not."

Tim had gotten up and stomped to the door. "Don't try to philosophize this away, Melinda. The fact is, you betrayed me. It's not something that a tearful apology is going to cure." He'd taken a long look around her room. His eyes had finally come to rest on her hunched-over figure on the bed. "Hey, happy Valentine's Day."

After she closed the door he had stood in the hall, paralyzed. Over his jagged breathing, he'd heard Melinda move inside the room. The sound of numbers being punched into a phone had turned his heart to stone. He had pressed his ear to the door and heard her guilty-sounding voice.

"George? It's me."

Tim had turned and fled down the hall.

•   •   •

Cars were parked up and down Caroline Henry's block. Tim squeezed his huge Oldsmobile between two compact cars and jogged past the nine houses between his car and the Henrys'. From a distance, he saw men in tuxedos walking in next to well-dressed women. *Great,* he thought. *I'm probably the only single guy here tonight.* He'd have to spend the whole evening talking to some well-meaning aunt who wanted to set him up on a blind date.

The rows of chairs were filling up fast as Tim made his way into the backyard. He slid into a chair toward the middle of the rows and leaned his head back to look at the sky. It was the half hour before real darkness. The sky had turned almost purple and in the distance the sun was a semicircle of orange. Tim sought out the first star of the night and made a silent wish. *Please, let me have fun tonight. For just a few hours, I wish that I could be freed from Melinda's grip.*

He looked around him, hoping he'd find someone he wanted to talk to. The first person who caught his eye was Tina Wollman, sitting three rows in front of him. *Ugh.* She was the type of girl he studiously avoided. To his right, he recognized one of the college cheerleaders. Cindy? Kiki? She was blabbing on and on about some sorority party she'd been to the night before. How much worse could it get?

There had to be someone. He just wasn't looking hard enough. As Ollie had pointed out, Caroline

Henry's wedding should be full of beautiful women. Tim studied the girls around him and gave a mental shrug. Sure, they were attractive. But that just wasn't enough.

When the organ music started, the chatter around him subsided like a quiet sigh. He turned his head to see the maid of honor make her way down the aisle.

Tim heard his own sharp intake of breath. The girl floated down the aisle in a long pink gown. Her eyes seemed to send out laser beams as she looked from side to side, smiling. Tim forced himself to shut his gaping mouth.

His stare took in every detail. His fingers ached with the longing to touch her ash-blond hair. He ran his finger down the list of names on the wedding program. *Megan Henry,* he said silently. Who was she? Caroline's sister? Cousin?

Every step brought her closer to Tim's aisle seat. His eyes were glued to her face. There was something familiar in her walk. Or was it the way she held her head? Had he seen her around campus? *No, I would've remembered,* he thought.

For a brief moment her eyes locked with his. He sensed, more than saw, the slight change of expression on her face. Oliver's words echoed in his mind: "If you open your eyes, you might see something you like." Tim smiled to himself. *Oh, I see something I like, Ollie. In fact, I have this strange feeling I see someone I could love.*

Twelve

"Ladies and gentlemen, I present Rick and Caroline Honan," the minister announced. Tim tore his eyes away from the wedding party and scanned the smiling crowd around him. Everybody was hugging and kissing like crazy. *I guess weddings really bring out the romance in people,* he thought. This particular ceremony had definitely awakened dormant emotions in him.

Tim allowed himself to follow Megan Henry's graceful descent from the makeshift altar where she'd stood during the wedding. As she turned her head to say something in the ear of the groomsman she'd come down the aisle with, the soft white lights overhead caught the highlights in her hair.

"Are you going to sit there all day?" a voice inquired. "Or do you want to join the party?"

Tim gave Robert Thorton a sheepish grin. "Hi, Rob. Guess I'm a little out of it," he said to his soccer coach.

Robert raised his eyebrows. "A little? I was about to put a mirror under your mouth to make sure you were still breathing." He laughed at his own joke and clapped Tim on the back.

"As you can see, I'm alive and well." Tim stood up and shook out his stiff legs.

"Good. Rick and I wouldn't want our star soccer player comatose on this happy occasion."

Before Tim could stop himself, words forced themselves from his brain to his throat, then out his mouth. "Do you know Megan Henry?" he asked. "She's the bridesmaid over there," he added, pointing to where Meg was talking with an older woman.

Robert looked across the lawn. "Her last name's Henry? Well, Rick mentioned that one of Caroline's young cousins was in the wedding. But she doesn't look so young."

Tim reached up to loosen his tie. Ever since he'd seen *her* he'd felt sort of out of breath. "No. She doesn't look young at all. She's got to be at least my age. Maybe older."

Robert laughed and pushed back his thinning strawberry-blond hair. "From the ridiculous tone in your voice, I'm wagering that you plan to find out her personal data yourself."

Tim felt his ears turning a little pink. "I don't know. Maybe."

His face fell in disappointment as Meg moved away from the crowd and into the house. Once her pale pink dress swished through the side door, Tim's view of the party seemed agonizingly bleak. "You don't think she's leaving, do you?" Tim asked, turning his head to look at Robert.

But Robert had disappeared. Tim shook his head from side to side. He felt like an idiot. How long had he been standing there staring into outer space? *Wilson, you'd better get your act together if you want to make any kind of impression on Megan*, he thought. *Scratch that. If you want to make any kind of* good *impression.*

Tim realized that he'd been talking to himself as if he were actually going to make an effort to *speak* to her. As if going up to a pretty girl and making conversation was the most natural thing in the world. Well, it was natural. Or at least it had been. Before Melinda.

Melinda. For the first time in almost two hours, her face materialized before his eyes. He forced the image to evaporate and checked his watch. It had been one hundred and fifteen minutes since he'd thought of her. Since their breakup—rather, her breakup—his best record for keeping Mel out of his mind had been thirty-three minutes. And that had been during a grueling round of sprints at one of his first track practices.

"Timothy Wilson, you look like you've seen a ghost." Tina Wollman's sickly sweet voice brought Tim out of his haze.

"Uh, hi, Tina. How are you?" Tim let out a silent groan. Tina was one of those girls who always accosted him after a game; she was pretty, but she had the personality of a barracuda.

"Just fine, *now.*" Tina stepped closer to Tim. She was so near he could feel her hot breath on his neck.

"Good, good. I'm glad to hear it." Tim's eyes sought out Megan in the crowd. If she'd left, he might as well go home.

"I didn't know you were going to be here. Are you bride or groom?"

"Guest." Tim edged away from Tina. She had put her hand on his arm, and her bright red nails looked like bloodstains on his dark jacket.

Tina giggled. "You are *so* funny. What I meant was, are you a guest of the bride or the groom?"

"I was kidding," Tim answered, giving her a thin smile. "Rick is my assistant soccer coach. He invited me."

"That's right! Silly me. I guess I was so entranced with your rippling muscles at the games that I didn't notice anybody else." She fluttered her eyelashes. Tim observed that there was a piece of fuzzy white lint clinging to her mascara.

"Yeah, well. Now you know," he said flatly. He'd been polite enough. Somewhere out there was Megan Henry. And if he didn't find her, some other guy would. "It's been great seeing you, Tina. Maybe we can talk later." Tim spun around and walked away. "Hey, how about a dance after dinner?" she called after him.

"Uh, sure," he mumbled over his shoulder. *If I don't suddenly develop a sprained ankle*, he added silently.

As Tim headed for the table of hors d'oeuvres, the back of his neck began to tingle. He glanced sharply to the left. Megan was standing next to a huge pile of gifts, and when he caught sight of her, he could have sworn that her head turned almost imperceptibly away. Had she been watching him?

Maybe Ollie was right. The past was over. It just might be time to move on.

• • •

Tim walked among the round tables that had been set up under the large tent, looking for his name on one of the cards that had been placed beside each plate. Tina's card caught his attention immediately. He quickly established that he hadn't been put at her table, and he breathed a sigh of relief.

His heart stopped when he saw *Megan Henry* written in gold lettering on one of the place cards. Tim looked intently at the cards on either side of hers. On the right was John Kingsley. Tim mentally ran his finger down the wedding program. John was the guy Meg had walked down the aisle with. He'd seen them talking, but the conversation hadn't seemed too intense, and a few minutes later Tim had seen the same guy put his arm around Kate Lyon's waist. Air flowed back into his lungs. Kingsley shouldn't be a problem.

Tim moved to the left and peered at the name card. *Timothy Wilson*. "Yes!" he whispered fiercely, and pumped his fist in victory. A few water glasses wobbled dangerously, and Tim put out a shaky hand to steady their thin stems.

Tim took a deep breath and shook his head. He was getting ahead of himself—way ahead. He'd sworn off girls for at least the next decade, maybe his whole life. If he allowed himself to get psyched because a pretty blonde was sitting next to him at dinner, then he was leaving himself open to any number of disasters—such as a broken heart.

Then again, he'd promised Ollie, and himself, that he'd try to get out of his funk. If he simply took the night for what it was, maybe he could have a few laughs. After all, he wasn't dead, he was just in hibernation from love.

Tim planned what he was going to say to Megan. Should he play it cool? Maybe pull a macho routine? Oliver always seemed to opt for plain old obnoxious, but that would never be Tim's style. He was going back and forth in his mind when Meg suddenly appeared before him.

Tim swallowed hard and wiped his palm surreptitiously on his tuxedo pants. "Hi, I'm Tim Wilson." *Okay, Wilson. You can still go either way on the macho strategy.*

Her response was a blur. Great. If he asked her to repeat the very first words of their conversation, she was going to think she was talking to either Beavis or Butt-head.

"I noticed you during the wedding," he heard himself say. "Your march was great. I mean, a lot of girls go down the aisle so fast, and you didn't. You . . ." Tim's words trailed off as he looked into her huge brown eyes. *So much for playing it cool,* he thought ruefully.

But she wasn't laughing at him. She wasn't arching her eyebrows or rolling her eyes the way Melinda used to. She was smiling and gracefully unfolding her napkin in her lap. *I can do this,* Tim realized. *If I let myself relax, I might actually enjoy myself.*

Tim barely tasted the chicken that was served for dinner. His mind was racing with questions he wanted to ask Meg: What was her favorite color?

Did she want to travel the world? What were her friends like? Had she ever been in a serious relationship? Did she like chocolate chip pancakes?

When she'd told him she was a freshman at Vermillion, he realized why he hadn't seen her around campus. *I knew I couldn't have been in that much of a fog this year,* he said to himself as a waiter set a plate of cherries jubilee in front of him.

"Can I count on you to dance with me after our coffee?" Tim asked Meg with a grin.

"Hmm. Let me just check my dance card to see if I still have some open slots," she answered, giggling. "Isn't that what they do in Jane Austen's books?"

"Jeez!" Gloria called across the table. "Are you two talking about Jane Austen? First it was dubbing versus subtitles, now it's classic literature. Have you ever heard of having fun?"

Tim thought he saw Meg's face turn a little pink. "There's nothing wrong with intelligent conversation," she answered Gloria.

"We were just about to start a discussion of Plato's ideal image of beauty," Tim joked to the table. "Anyone care to join us?"

Gloria took a bite of her dessert and stared at them. Hadn't she ever seen anyone flirt before? "Sorry, Tim. I guess I'm just not used to Meg being out of high school. Of course, she's always been ahead of her years."

"Gloria, do you mind?" Meg sounded slightly irritated.

"I'm just bragging about you, Meg. Accept it with grace." Gloria turned to Tim. "Tim, did you know

Meg was valedictorian of her high school? She gave the most wonderful graduation speech—"

"C'mon, Gloria," Meg said.

Tim loved the way Meg was modest about her accomplishments. "That's so weird," he said. "I spoke at my graduation, too. What did you talk about?"

"Oh, you know, the usual stuff," she answered vaguely. "Hey. Gloria's right. Let's do less talking and more partying. How about that dance?" She looked at an imaginary wristwatch. "I have an open spot right about . . . now!" she added.

Tim stood up and bowed deeply. "It would be my pleasure, ma'am." He held out his hand, and Meg took it. A warm shiver ran up his arm to his shoulder.

Please, he prayed, *don't let me step on her toes!*

"Mind if I cut in?" a deep voice said.

Tim opened his eyes and looked around. What kind of idiot would interrupt two people who were obviously enjoying their dance together? He was about to politely tell the guy to get lost when Meg responded to the offer.

"Hi, Dad! I'd love to dance," she said, stepping quickly away from Tim.

Close call, Tim thought. *That could have been ugly.*

Tim turned and saw Meg's father giving him the once-over. Mr. Henry gave him a bland, good-natured smile and danced away with Meg. *He looks like a nice guy,* Tim thought. He imagined going to Sunday dinner at Meg's parents' house. He'd go pick her up at her dorm and they'd walk hand in hand up to the front door of her childhood house. After meat loaf and mashed potatoes, Meg would show him her old room. He pictured the room with flowered wallpaper and some worn stuffed animals on the bed. Maybe they'd look through her old high school yearbooks. . . .

Alarm bells started going off in his head as he saw Tina walking straight toward him. It was obviously no use to pretend he hadn't seen her. She was waving and speeding up into a trot. He plastered a smile on his face and waited for the assault.

"Tim, the night's almost over and you haven't asked me for one dance," she greeted him in a baby voice. "You'd better make good on your promise."

Meg was still dancing with her father. They were all the way on the other side of the floor, near the band. He was stuck. "Do you want to dance?" he asked, hoping she'd notice the lack of enthusiasm in his voice.

"I'd love to!" Tina answered, shoving herself into his arms.

Tim made a point of keeping about a foot of space between their bodies as he moved with her in time to the music. Tina only came up to the middle of his chest, and when she looked up at him, he could see into her nostrils. He felt like a robot, mechanically answering her questions while he planned a means of escape.

Several couples away, Meg leaned past her father's shoulder and gave Tim a dazzling smile. He responded by glancing down at Tina's platinum-blond head and grimacing. Meg winked, then tilted her face back toward her dad.

"Tim, hello, hello. You're a million miles away," Tina practically shouted in his ear. "Aren't you having fun?"

"Sorry, Tina. I, uh, have a cramp in my foot. I didn't want to spoil our dance, but I think I'd better sit the rest of this one out."

"Okay." Tina pouted. "But if I see you waltzing with some other girl, I'm going to cut in."

Tim groaned as he walked as quickly as he could off the dance floor. He made a beeline for Rick and Caroline, who were sipping champagne at a nearby table. "Hi, you two. Congratulations!" he said when he got within earshot.

Rick stood up and shook Tim's hand, then pulled him closer for a fast hug. "Thanks, man. I'm glad you could come."

"It's been one of the best nights of my life," Tim answered.

"Hey, do you know Caroline?" Rick asked, dropping his arm around Caroline's shoulders.

"We've met a few times," Caroline said, holding her hand out to Tim. "I noticed you've been keeping my cousin occupied tonight, Tim. Thanks a lot. I was afraid she might get bored."

Were they actually *thanking* him for dancing with Meg? "Believe me, it's been my pleasure. I'd gladly keep her company *every* night."

Caroline let out a laugh, while Rick reached over and ruffled his hair. "You're sweet, Tim," Caroline said. "I'll tell Meg you said that. She'll be thrilled."

I sure hope so, Tim responded silently.

•   •   •

Tim stood on the Henrys' front lawn, staring at Meg from a distance. He was trying to remember how depressed he'd been earlier that afternoon, but it was impossible. He felt better than he had in months, maybe years. And there was no going back—he hoped.

Meg was holding Caroline's bouquet and talking with one of the other bridesmaids. He thought he saw her frown as she walked away from the other girl and drifted in his direction. Her face seemed to light up when she saw him striding toward her. He reached out to clasp her hand and pulled her gently away from the other guests. "Let's get away from all the noise," he whispered.

She nodded, and he led her to the edge of the dark lawn. They stood in the shadow of a tree, and it seemed that the rest of the party had faded into the background. He cleared his throat a couple of times. He wanted to express what he was feeling, but no words in the English language seemed appropriate. *Too bad I don't know a Romance language,* he thought. *Maybe the Italians have a really good way to say, "I think I might love you."*

"Tonight has been really great," he said finally. "I think it's going to be forever imprinted on my brain." It wasn't the most clever thing to say, but at least she wasn't looking at him as if he were crazy.

". . . had an amazing time, too," he heard her say. Why was it that every time she spoke he was so mesmerized by her eyes that he couldn't concentrate on her words?

He decided the solution was to stop talking and take action. He pushed her gently against the wooden fence behind them and bent his head so that his lips were just an inch from hers. Moments later, she closed the space. Her lips were soft and warm under his, and Tim had the sensation he was floating on a cloud. As he closed his eyes and pressed his body more tightly against hers, a surprising thought flashed across his mind: Kissing Melinda had never felt this right.

Thirteen

Tim's clock-radio started blasting classic rock at nine o'clock Sunday morning. The music was followed by the insistent buzz of a backup travel alarm clock he kept on his nightstand. Tim woke with a start, trying to discern whether he was at a Rolling Stones concert or in the parking lot of the police station. He sat up and shut off both alarms with his fist.

On the other side of the room, Oliver was still sound asleep. "That guy probably slept through Hurricane Andrew," Tim muttered as he fell back on the bed. He reached back with one hand and plumped the pillow under his head. Bright morning sun filtered into the room and a cool breeze fluttered the half-drawn shade. From his bed, Tim could see his slightly rumpled tuxedo jacket hanging over the closet doorknob. He rubbed his eyes and let the memories of the night before come flooding back.

Megan. Dancing. The kiss. He smiled as he remembered the sweetness of her lips against his. How long had it lasted? A minute? An hour? When he closed his eyes again, he could still see the glow of the white lights from the wedding reception in the distance. "What a night." He sighed happily.

A surge of adrenaline coursed through his veins as he got up to take a shower. For the first time in months, he hadn't woken from an anguished dream about Melinda. Grateful that Ollie was snoring contentedly, he danced a jig to the bathroom.

The stream of hot water from the shower cleared the last remnants of sleep from his head, and he improvised a blues song as he rubbed a bar of soap over his lean torso. "I found a girl named Meg, and I want to make her mine," he sang. "She's as lovely as a rose, and everything about her's fine . . ." He laughed at the silly words reverberating against the bathroom tiles. "Oh, baby. Oh, baby, you're so very, so very fine . . ." he continued, scrubbing shampoo through his hair.

A loud banging on the door interrupted his second chorus. "What's going on in there?" Ollie shouted. "You sound like you're in pain!"

Tim turned off the water and wrapped a relatively fresh towel around his waist. He poked his head out of the shower and grinned at his roommate. Oliver's strawberry-blond hair was sticking straight up, and from the look on his face, he wasn't happy about being awake. "Come on, Ollie. Haven't you ever heard somebody singing in the shower?"

"You call that singing?" Oliver put his hands over his ears and made a face.

"Yes, singing. The verb *to sing*. From the Latin root *singus bluesamus*. As in singin' the blues. Even though I'm happy. Got it?" Tim pulled on a pair of green-and-white striped boxers and rubbed his hair with the damp towel.

"I've got it, but I sure don't want it. Is this your way of getting back at me for not cleaning my side of the room?"

Tim rolled up the towel and flicked it against Ollie's shoulder. "You spend the last three months complaining that I'm depressed all the time, and now that I'm literally *singing* my good cheer, you think I'm punishing you?" Tim laughed and took another swipe at Oliver.

Oliver held up his hands in surrender. "Okay. I give up. Why are you so annoyingly happy at this *extremely* early hour of the morning?"

"Two words, man—*Megan Henry*." Tim went to his dresser and pulled out a pair of black track shorts.

Oliver stared at Tim, his mouth wide open. "Are you telling me this is because of a *girl*?" He looked up at the ceiling and held his hands together. "O God above, thank you for delivering my roommate from his state of post-girlfriend melancholia."

"Don't be a jerk," Tim said, digging his running shoes out from under the bed.

"A jerk? Are you kidding? This is incredible. I knew that wedding was going to work some magic!"

"Well, for once in your life, Staley, you were one hundred percent right—at least I hope you were."

"So who is she?"

"Her name's Meg. She's Caroline's cousin."

"Dude, nice work. If she looks anything like Caroline, she must be a babe."

"She is. And then some."

"How come I don't know who she is? Does she go to the university, or what?" Oliver lounged on his bed, combing his fingers through the tangles in his hair.

"She's a freshman at Vermillion."

"So she's got looks *and* a brain. That's an unusual combination in a woman."

"Shut up, Ollie. You're really a sexist pig, you know that?" Tim walked around the room, picking up the various pieces of his rented tuxedo. "Sometimes I'm embarrassed to admit I know you!"

"Keep your track shorts on, Wilson. I'm just teasing."

"You're not funny."

"Before you get self-righteous on me, let me refresh your memory. Yesterday you were stomping around this room talking about how all girls were either superficial or manipulative—or both."

"Did I say that?" Tim gazed out the window for a moment. It was impossible to imagine using either of those adjectives to describe Meg. "I guess I was feeling pretty bitter."

"When are you gonna see her next?"

"Who, Meg?"

"No, Mother Teresa! Of course Meg."

"I don't know. First I have to get up the courage to call her."

Oliver raised his eyebrows. "You'd better get

some guts, bro. Fast. If she's really worth all that wailing in the shower, there are probably guys waiting in line to ask her out."

Tim groaned. "Don't worry, I'll call."

Oliver got off his bed and scooped up Tim's discarded wet towel. "Mind if I use this?"

Tim shook his head. "Forget what I said about you being a sexist pig, Ollie. You're just a pig, period."

"Oink, oink," Oliver responded. He shut the bathroom door behind him. A few seconds later, Tim could hear his roommate over the sound of the shower. "Oh baby, oh baby, you're so fine," he was singing in a high, cracking voice.

"If Meg believes in judging a man by his friends," Tim said aloud, "I'm doomed."

The sun was hot on Tim's back as he stretched out before his race on Sunday afternoon. He leaned over and touched his toes, bouncing up and down to loosen the muscles of his back. He flexed his left foot and felt the familiar pull in his calf as the muscle stretched. Along with a couple of other guys on the team, he was running the two-mile. It was an exhausting race, and he wanted to make sure that his legs didn't cramp up in the middle of it. He hoped that he hadn't jinxed himself by lying to Tina about having a foot cramp while they were dancing at the reception.

He was still thinking about the feigned foot cramp when a pair of bare legs appeared before him, blocking the sun. Tim's heart jumped. "Meg?" he said, standing up.

"Guess again," Tina Wollman said, smiling up at him. She was wearing a pair of short denim cut-offs and a bright orange halter top.

Tim's heart dropped. Of course Meg wouldn't be there. He hadn't even mentioned to her that he had a track meet that day. "Hi, Tina."

"Hi right back at you, Tim. Have fun last night?"

"Yeah. It was a nice wedding."

"You must be tired after all that dancing you did with the little maid of honor." Tina put her hands on her hips, waiting for his response.

Tim let out a nervous laugh. "Oh well, you know how it is." It wasn't a direct answer, but at least he'd said *something*.

"I never figured you as a guy interested in sophomores. I didn't know that was your style," she sneered.

"You mean Meg?" Tim asked. He looked at Tina's nodding head and noticed that her eyebrows were disappearing into her bangs. "She's not a sophomore. She's a freshman."

"Oh, a *freshman*. Even better. Well, different strokes, I guess."

"Uh, yeah." What was this girl's problem? Had she been out in the sun too long, or was she just terminally ditzy?

"Well, I've gotta go. I promised Barry Milburn that I'd watch him run." It sounded like good-bye, but she stayed glued to the spot.

Tim leaned over and continued stretching. If he ignored her, maybe she'd go away. After almost a minute, he heard her loud sigh as she walked away, kicking up dust behind her. Tim looked up and breathed a sigh of relief. Then he laughed. Poor Barry was really in for it.

Tim scanned the field. Rationally, he knew that Meg wouldn't be there. Irrationally, he told himself there was always a chance. Squinting, he held a hand above his eyes to shield them from the sun. As usual, not too many spectators had shown up for the Sunday meet. A few parents were scattered along the track, but most students were somewhere on campus recovering from their Saturday night.

There was no sign of Meg. *What's she doing right now?* Tim wondered. He tried to picture her eating brunch with her friends or studying in Vermillion's old stone library. Was she thinking about him? Was she wishing she hadn't written her phone number down on that paper cocktail napkin? Tim's heart sank at the thought. *Get it together, Tim,* he said to himself. He looked at his digital wristwatch. *In about five minutes, you have to run a two-mile race.* He was already behind schedule. He normally spent at least fifteen minutes mentally psyching himself up for a race. Even Melinda's dumping him hadn't kept him from maintaining that ritual.

He closed his eyes and inhaled deeply, trying to visualize the finish line of his race. Instead, an image of the back of Meg's head as she'd walked down the aisle the night before appeared before him. He rubbed his temples and forced his mind to become blank. Almost instantly the previous mental picture was replaced with one of Melinda's mocking face the night he'd surprised her in her dorm room. Finally Tim opened his eyes with a shudder. His concentration was shot. The thought of the searing pain Mel had inflicted on him dampened his happiness about having met Meg. *Is Melinda going to have this hold over me forever?* he wondered desperately.

"Yo, Wilson. Get over here and line up for the race," Coach Edelman shouted.

Tim crossed his fingers for luck and jogged to his spot. He nodded to the other runners and quickly assumed his starting position, knees slightly bent and one foot in front of the other.

"On your mark!" the starter yelled.

Tim felt the tension of the last few months well up inside of him.

"Get set!" the man's voice boomed.

Tim had an overwhelming urge to fling the last remnants of Melinda out of his system. He was angry that memories of her were intruding on his life. He was angry that the way she'd treated him had made him suspicious of girls' motives in general. Most of all, he was furious that he'd wasted the entire semester feeling lousy about the fact that she'd let him down. Tim's blood was pounding, and his feet itched to take off from the starting line.

At the sound of the gun, Tim's feet flew into action. He didn't pace himself. He didn't notice the position of the other runners. He put one foot in front of the other, faster and faster, racing away from his history with Melinda. As he circled the track again and again, he heard the distant sound of cheering. He whizzed by Tina's orange halter top, and then the astonished face of his coach. With every step, his mind cleared and his heart soared.

Tim lost count of the number of times he'd gone around the track. His lungs cried out for oxygen and the muscles in his legs ached almost unbearably. He pressed forward. Suddenly he became aware that his name was being shouted by several different people. He tried to ignore the distraction, but Coach Edelman's voice became louder and more insistent. "Wilson," the coach shouted, "snap out of it!"

Tim continued running but took a moment to glance over his shoulder. His teammates were waving their arms wildly, motioning him to return to the group. Tim slowed down and moved his gaze all the way around the track. The other runners had stopped. They were all standing on the sidelines, either gulping down water or staring at his lone figure. *What's going on?* he wondered. *Why did they stop the race?*

He came to an abrupt halt. Sweat dripped off his face and onto the ground, making dark spots in the gray dust all around him. He staggered forward, the full effects of his overexertion finally catching up with him. A wave of dizziness swept through him, and he knelt on the ground, keeping his head bent low.

Through a haze of nausea, he felt Coach Edelman's hand grip his shoulder. "Tim, are you okay?" His voice sounded uncharacteristically gentle as he bent to look into Tim's eyes.

"Sure, Coach," Tim wheezed. "But what happened with the race? I thought I was making pretty good time."

"What do you mean, what happened? You won!"

"What? I won?" Tim stood up, his heartbeat slowing down to somewhere near its normal rate.

"Wilson, you didn't just win. You beat your own best time by almost a whole minute! Didn't you know?"

"No . . . I didn't even realize the race was over." Tim gave the coach a smile. "I guess I was really in la-la land."

"Well, congratulations. You just moved into the number-one spot on the team. We haven't had a freshman do that since the early eighties." Coach Edelman put a hand on Tim's arm and guided him back to the rest of the team.

Tim remained distracted as he accepted high-fives from the rest of his teammates. What had just happened? He felt like he was coming down to earth after an out-of-body experience. The last fifteen minutes had been akin to one of those rebirthing experiences he'd read about in psychology class. He felt totally drained, but exhilarated. *Good riddance, Melinda,* he thought. *My new life is about to begin.*

It was late Sunday night. Tim had given up trying to study after a useless hour in the library and returned to his room to contemplate calling Meg. Carefully he transferred her phone number from the shredded napkin to his address book. His index finger traced a delicate line over each of the seven digits. Should he call that night? It was a tantalizing thought. He imagined holding the phone and hearing Meg's voice in his ear.

But it was too soon. What would he say? He couldn't tell her that he'd had his best track meet ever because anger at his ex-girlfriend had spurred him to victory. And he couldn't tell her that Oliver wanted to know if she had a good-looking room-mate so they could double-date. What if she didn't want to hear from him at all? Maybe she was in another guy's arms right that second, laughing about how she'd danced with some jock at her cousin's wedding.

Tim sighed heavily. At least when he'd been depressed about Melinda, he'd known how to feel every second of the day—terrible. Now he was on an emotional roller coaster. One second he felt so elated he wanted to hug everyone he saw. A minute later he'd feel tears threatening at the thought that he might never see Meg again.

If I call her tonight, he realized, *it's guaranteed that I'll be so tongue-tied I'll make a fool of myself.* If he waited until the next day, he'd be calmer. And he'd have had almost a full forty-eight hours of believing that he was about to experience some-thing special. He slapped his book shut and turned out the light.

Moonlight shone in through the open window, creating crazy patterns of shadows on his walls. Tim shut his eyes and wished that someday Meg would be there beside him. He could see her laughing and making shadow animals in the moonlight. "Good night, Megan Henry," he whis-pered.

Fourteen

"If you stare at that phone long enough, it might bite you," Oliver said Monday night. He dropped his backpack on the floor and did a belly flop onto his bed.

"I'm thinking hard and just *happen* to be looking in the direction of the phone," Tim responded. "And hello to you, too," he added.

"You don't actually expect me to believe that, do you?" Ollie asked, grinning. "Tim, you are pathetic. Just call the girl."

Inwardly Tim sighed. He'd been hoping that Ollie wouldn't come back from the library until late. Now his roommate was going to make a big deal about Tim's calling Meg. He might even insist on sticking around to listen. "Easy for you to say." Not the snappiest comeback, but he had a lot on his mind.

"Easy for me to *do*, you mean." Oliver moved the phone away from Tim and sat down on one of their desk chairs. He picked up the receiver. "Just watch and learn, friend."

"You're not calling Meg!" Tim shouted.

"Dude, you need a lesson in mellow." Oliver laughed. "Of course I'm not calling Meg. I'm calling Suzanne."

"Who's Suzanne?"

"While you were waltzing with Meg Henry at the reception on Saturday night, I was slam-dancing with a gorgeous brunette named Suzanne Rogers at the Beta house. Now be quiet."

Tim watched as Ollie dialed Suzanne's number and casually asked her for a date Saturday night. From Ollie's end of the conversation, it didn't sound like she remembered exactly who Oliver was, but she finally said yes to the date. Ollie hung up the phone with a satisfied smirk on his face.

"Was that brilliant, or what?" Oliver took a bow in the middle of the room.

"Is it my imagination, or did Suzanne have no idea who you were?" Tim asked.

"Who cares if she didn't?" Oliver retorted. "The point is, I charmed her into going out with me Saturday night. I'll take the rest from there."

Tim fell back on his bed, laughing. "I've gotta hand it to you. You're brave."

"Thanks. Now it's your turn." Oliver regarded Tim with a steady stare.

"Fine. I'll call. I was going to, anyway," Tim said, reaching for the phone. "Why don't you go watch the tube in the lounge or something?"

"Don't want your roomie around to hear you whispering sweet nothings to the lady, huh?"

"Something like that." Tim mentally willed Oliver to leave the room.

Oliver stuck a Kansas City Royals cap on his head and walked over to the door. "I'll be back in twenty minutes. Use the time wisely."

Tim picked up the phone and took a deep breath. Why was he so nervous? *It's not like I've never called a girl before,* he said to himself. But he wasn't just calling a girl—he was calling *Meg.* What if she didn't want to hear from him? Or what if he called and realized that she was just like the rest of the uninspiring women in his life?

He'd been in a pretty strange frame of mind on Saturday night. He might have romanticized Meg in his mind. Music and good food could have that effect. Then again, it had been two days, and he still wanted to talk to her more than he wanted to breathe.

He'd memorized her phone number a hundred times over. He probably could have recited it backward if he had to. "Here goes nothing," he said to the Miles Davis poster over his desk.

She picked up on the first ring. "What now?" Her voice sounded distinctly irritated.

Instead of feeling alarmed, Tim laughed. Meg definitely had a unique style. "Are you always this friendly, or are you in training to be the world's worst receptionist?" he asked.

The conversation went uphill from there. It wasn't exactly what he'd planned—he didn't pull off Oliver's cool—but it was far from a disaster. Tim wanted to punch himself for having waited so long to call her.

When Ollie didn't show up after twenty minutes, Tim breathed a sigh of relief. It looked as if his roommate had found something to do that was even more fun than torturing Tim.

"I have an away track meet Friday night," Tim finally said to Meg. "But how about going out Saturday?"

"I'd love to," she answered.

Tim's heartbeat picked up its pace, and he could see his silly grin in the mirror over the dresser. "Great." Tim didn't know where to go from there. He hadn't thought past asking her out. And he hadn't actually been on a date since he'd arrived at the university.

The neon sign above Moody's Diner flashed in his mind. It was neutral territory. She probably went there all the time with friends.

"How about starting at Moody's for breakfast?" he asked.

"Moody's Diner?" she asked.

"Is there another Moody's that I don't know about?" Suddenly an image of a Moody's Adult Video Store or Moody's House of Massage popped into his mind.

"No," she answered. "Moody's is perfect."

"How about if I pick you up at ten?"

There was a pause on Meg's end of the line. He could hear her soft breathing. "Why don't we meet there? I'll have a couple of errands to run that morning."

"Whatever works for you, Meg," he answered.

"You can appear on a unicycle, for all I care. I just can't wait to see you."

Her laughter was like a light at the end of a dark tunnel. "Sweet dreams," she whispered. There was a quiet click and Tim remained still, listening to the sound of the dial tone.

Now, he thought, *I just have to figure out where we're going to go after Moody's!* He looked around the room. Where was Ollie when he really needed him?

Tim opened the passenger door of his car and waited for Meg to slide in. As he walked around to his side of the Oldsmobile he gave himself a pep talk. *Okay, Wilson. The diner went over pretty well. Conversation was good, and she didn't gag when she saw you. Just pray that she likes roller coasters!*

"Where to?" Meg asked brightly.

"How do you feel about roller coasters?" He noticed her face pale visibly.

"You mean aside from my deathly fear of heights?"

"Uh-oh. I guess the amusement park outside of town is a no-go!" He quickly racked his brain. Why didn't he have a plan B? In the movies, the guy always had a plan B.

Meg laughed. "An amusement park sounds great! Just don't be surprised if I put a steel grip on your arm."

The light from Meg's eyes made her whole face glow. Tim's lips ached to touch hers; the memory of their last kiss was burning a hole in his brain. Tim edged across the car seat and ran a hand down her silky cheek. His heart pounded as she reached up and put her arms around his neck. For some reason, kissing her during the day was even more exciting than it had been at night. He had to force himself to pull away and start the car.

Meg rolled down her window and stuck her head out. "Onward, James!" she shouted. "To the carnival."

The sun had just started to sink in the sky. Shades of pink and purple were spreading out along the horizon, highlighting the puffy white clouds in the distance. The game booths and rides of Sam's Big World of Fun were painted all the colors of the rainbow, and garish lights covered every available inch of wood and steel. Tim and Meg had walked all over the amusement park, eating mustard-covered corn dogs and chewy homemade taffy. Meg had insisted they watch a twenty-minute-long pickle-eating contest, and Tim had cheered with her when a twelve-year-old boy had beaten his older—and much fatter—opponents.

In the sweet-smelling night air, they stood close together, waiting to experience Sam's main attraction—Thunder Mountain. Meg's grip on his hand got tighter and tighter as they inched their way forward in the line. Without thinking, Tim hugged Meg's body close. The material of her tight shirt was warm under his hands, and he could feel her heart beating against his chest. He smiled to the world at large, enjoying the sight of other couples in line holding hands and kissing. Ollie had been right: Second to weddings, amusement parks were at the top of the list of romantic atmospheres.

"You know, Thunder Mountain is one of the few remaining wooden roller coasters in the United States," he said when their turn on the ride finally came.

"Wonderful. I'll think about splintering wood while we plunge down that first giant drop!" she answered. She was staring up at the monster structure, biting her lip and wringing the loose material of his shirt.

"You'll see. The second the ride's over you'll be begging me to get right back in line." A high school kid wearing overalls and no shirt held up the chain they were standing behind and motioned them forward.

Meg shot him a withering look. "Care to bet on that? Say, loser has to go on that rickety-looking Tilt-a-Whirl two times in a row?"

"You're on. I just hope you have a strong stomach."

They were in the front car of the roller coaster. Meg seemed to be holding her breath as she buckled her seat belt and pulled it tight across her lap. *I hope she doesn't hate me forever over this one,* Tim thought when the attendant flipped the switch and the roller coaster came to life. As the car lurched forward Meg reached over and grabbed his hand. The sensation of her fingernails digging lightly into his skin sent shivers running up and down his spine. *Then again, it would be a shame to waste this opportunity.*

All logical thoughts were driven from his mind when they reached the top of the first steep hill. It seemed as if the amusement park was miles, rather than feet, below them. The people they'd been standing in line with looked like ants, their tiny open-mouthed faces tilted upward. He felt his breath being squeezed out of his lungs as their small car rolled slowly over the peak of the incline. "I'm going to get you for this, Tim Wilson," Meg said through gritted teeth in the second before the ride took them plummeting downward. It felt like free fall, and Tim lost touch with the hard seat beneath him.

Almost as soon as it had started, the drop was over. But their speed seemed to pick up as the ride hurtled onward. Tim screamed with Meg as the ride spiraled them faster and faster over the creaking wooden frame. Sky, clouds, lights, and people whizzed by in a crazy blur. Above the screams of other passengers, he could hear Meg's distinct and blood-curdling shriek.

The ride ground to a halt. They'd been on the roller coaster only ninety seconds, but their hair and faces had undergone a massive transformation. Meg turned to him. Her brown eyes were sparkling, and her long blond hair was loose and tangled around her face. "That was great! It felt like flying!" She unfastened her seat belt and sprang from the car.

Tim stood up slowly, wondering if she could tell that his legs were shaking. He stepped cautiously out of the ride, suspicious of the firm ground under him. "*Great* isn't the first word that comes to mind, but it'll do." He gave her a smile and reached up to rub his sweaty forehead.

Meg took his hand and pulled him back into the milling crowd of people. "If I weren't determined not to lose our bet, I might actually want to get back in line. Who knew that I was a closet roller coaster junkie?" She looked up at his face for a response, and her eyes widened. "Tim, are you okay? You're looking a little green."

"I'm fine, just fine. But how about we skip the Tilt-a-Whirl and take a nice relaxing ride on the Ferris wheel?"

Meg covered her mouth. A giggle squeaked out and she bent over, laughing. "This is what I like to see. A little nineties role reversal in action. You're acting like a *girl!*" She could barely get the words out, and Tim felt his face turn red.

"Let's chalk it up to gorging on too much taffy before those double loops," he begged.

Meg let out one last giggle. "Okay. Since you've been manly all day, I guess I can let this one inconsistency slip by."

"You've got a generous soul, Meg. So, can we put Thunder Mountain behind us and get in line for the Ferris wheel?"

Instead of answering, she put her arm around his waist and propelled him in the direction of the more gentle, romantic ride. "Now that I seem to have conquered my acrophobia, I'm actually looking forward to the view from the top of the wheel."

"Just promise not to rock our gondola!" Tim said, stepping into the cozy but insubstantial open-roofed compartment.

The huge wheel moved slowly, lifting them gently off the ground and into the air. *This is more like it*, Tim thought as they left the lights of the park below. The sky had turned midnight blue and, just like the Saturday before, the moon shone brightly overhead. He reached out for Meg, and she slid closer to him on the narrow seat. With one arm around her shoulders and one resting lightly along the back of their gondola, Tim bent his head and breathed in the lemony scent of Meg's hair. "Heaven must be something like this," he observed.

Beside him, Meg nodded and covered his knee with one delicate hand. "It's like the stars and the lights from Sam's are all blended together. I feel like we're going around and around in outer space." She paused and turned to look behind her. The gondola swung slightly, and she quickly faced forward again. "It's like we're the only people in the whole world," she whispered.

Tim forgot to worry about their precarious position, suspended from the steel wheel, and put both of his arms around Meg. He kissed her lightly in the hollow of her neck and then moved his lips to her earlobe. "Right now we *are* the only people in the whole world," he whispered back. At the apex of their ascent into the sky, he put a hand under Meg's chin and kissed her deeply.

They were still locked in an embrace when a loud voice instructed them to come up for air—the ride was over.

Tim shut the door to his room quietly behind him and stumbled his way over Oliver's various piles of junk until his hand hit the switch of his small bedside lamp. He sank down on his bed and kicked off his shoes. The day had been incredible. He'd only known Meg a week, and already the past felt like the distant pages of a history book.

On their way out of the amusement park, Meg had bought him a pink rose made of tissue paper. "One rose is worth a thousand words," she'd said, tucking the rose's stem into one of the buttonholes of his oxford-cloth shirt.

Tim ran his fingers over the tissue petals. He'd keep it forever. He opened the drawer of his nightstand to stash the flower safely away from Ollie's prying eyes. As he moved some papers to make room for it he uncovered his picture of Melinda. *Damn,* he thought. That photograph had a way of appearing when he was least in the mood to see it. Reluctantly he pulled out Melinda's smiling face.

Settling back against his pillows, he propped up the frame on his bed. It was strange, but somehow Melinda's face looked different. Her features were sharper, and her wide grin had the menacing quality of a pit bull's snarl. Was he hallucinating, or was that the real Melinda? Even the frame looked different; its shiny golden tint seemed cheap and tacky. Tim picked up the picture and put it in his lap for closer examination. He held the small lamp over his bed so that the light would shine directly on Melinda's face.

When he glanced back at the photo, another smile had taken the place of Melinda's. Blinking his eyes, Tim saw Meg's beautiful face staring up at him. Call it fate. Call it destiny. Call it crazy. Tim's heart now belonged utterly and completely to Megan Henry.

Fifteen

On Monday afternoon Tim elbowed through the student activities center, wondering if he'd make it to his mailbox in one piece. The building was packed with dripping-wet bodies. Whether they were cramming for an exam, eating a late lunch, or just hanging out, every student on campus seemed to have sought shelter from the rain in the humid, overcrowded space of Trenton Hall.

Tim dialed the combination of the lock on his mailbox and wondered if Meg was sitting somewhere in Vermillion's student center. Had she remembered an umbrella that morning? Was she wearing one of those bright yellow rain slickers that a lot of girls seemed to like? He'd never seen her in the rain. She probably looked great even with drops of water clinging to her eyelashes and running down her face.

"Hey, Tim, did you forget your combination or

are you trying to hold the rest of us hostage in this sardine can?"

Tim's daydream ended and he looked behind him. Jeff Gold smiled and gave him a playful punch on the shoulder. "Is it a bad mail day, or what?"

"Sorry, Jeff. I, uh, forgot my combination for a second. But it just came to me." Tim quickly opened his mailbox and fished around inside. He grabbed the contents and closed the door with a bang.

Jeff crammed in beside him. "Where were you Saturday night? The track team decided to get together and go for pizza, but we couldn't get hold of you all day."

"I was busy." He didn't feel like talking about his date with Meg. Somehow, relating the details of riding Thunder Mountain and the Ferris wheel would take away from how special it had been. *Jeez, I'm really turning into a cornball,* he realized.

"Too bad. Maybe next time." Jeff peered into the dark hole of his mailbox and groaned. "Of course, I get nothing but a notice for an overdue book. Why do I bother checking?"

Tim followed Jeff as he pushed his way through the swarming mass of students. As they walked Tim glanced through his meager pile of mail. There were a couple of flyers. One informed him that political science majors had to meet with their advisors to discuss the next year's course load. The other had a picture of a guy playing the saxophone: *Hey, jazz fans, don't miss this note!* it said in big, black letters.

Tim looked at the last piece of mail. When he saw the handwriting on the lavender stationery, his heart skipped a beat. It had been a few months, but he'd remember that long line over the capital *T* for the next twenty years. He quickly turned the envelope over to see the return address. As he expected, a large *M. W.* took up most of the back flap.

He and Jeff had reached the double glass front doors of Trenton Hall, and Jeff was looking at him expectantly. "Sorry, what did you say?" Tim asked distractedly.

"For the third time, do you want to go to my dorm and watch the baseball game?" Jeff scratched his head and imitated Tim's blank expression.

"Sorry. Uh, I've gotta go get a book from the library. But thanks." Tim turned and headed for the group of lounge chairs next to the student center's wall of windows.

"I thought you said you were going to the library!" Jeff called out after him.

"In a minute. First I need to check some notes." *And read this letter,* he added silently.

"All right, man, take it easy." Jeff put his windbreaker over his head and stepped out into the rain. Through the window, Tim could see him sprinting across campus, dodging around the many umbrella-carrying students in his path.

Tim spotted a girl with curly brown hair gathering up her books. He dashed to the chair she was sitting on so that he'd be poised to grab it when she left. But it took her a long time. First she looked through her backpack. She pulled out a brush and ran it through her hair. Then she took out some lip gloss and smoothed it over her mouth. Finally she seemed ready to go. But after getting halfway out of the chair she sat back down. Tim let out an exasperated sigh.

"*Sorry*," she said, looking up at him. "I just need to tie my *shoes*."

Tim mumbled an apology and tried to look patient. At last she picked up her backpack and took off for the doors. He plopped into the chair and held the lavender envelope with two fingers. *What do you want, Melinda?* he silently asked the letter. He briefly considered stuffing it into a nearby trash can, but instead he opened it.

His heart raced as he started to read her sprawling handwriting. It was so achingly familiar that he felt as if he'd been transported back to his senior year of high school.

Dear Tim,

I know you're mad at me—furious, probably—and I don't blame you. I've been a rotten girlfriend lately. You're probably reading this and wondering how I even have the gall to still call myself your girlfriend. But that's what I am. And I always will be. What happened with George was a huge mistake. I could never stop loving you, and finally I've admitted that to myself. I guess I was just scared and lonely without you. You can understand that, can't you? Anyway, I really need to see you. To make things right between us. Please give me another chance. I know you want to, even if you're too proud to admit it. That's all I can say in a stupid letter. CALL ME!

Love forever,
Mel

P.S. I've been dreaming about you every night. Remember our prom? Certain scenes keep coming back to me. In case you've forgotten (which I know you haven't), next time I see you I'll refresh your memory! Bye again.

Love,
Mel

Tim sat with the single piece of paper dangling from his fingertips. If he'd gotten that letter two weeks earlier—maybe even just a week earlier—he would have run to the nearest pay phone and dialed her number. But now he sat absolutely still, stone-faced. Who did she think she was? She didn't even mention the possibility that he might have met someone else. She didn't consider that he might have his own George.

He desperately wanted to hate her. He wanted to turn her into an object of scorn—or, even better, pity. But he couldn't. Not with the smell of her skin and her hair practically leaping off the page. *What now? Why now?* he asked himself. Mel must have some kind of ESP that told her he'd met Meg. Otherwise she'd never want him back. Would she?

Oblivious to the rain, Tim jogged back to his dorm. His head was pounding. He wished he *had* just thrown the letter away. He could have assumed it was some token note saying that she hoped he was holding up okay without her. Now a million unbidden thoughts were rushing through his brain. If only Melinda hadn't mentioned their prom night; it had been the best night of his life.

He stopped in his tracks, rain still pouring on his head. *It was the best night of my life—except for the two evenings I've spent with Megan*, he realized. That was it. All he needed to do was to be with Meg for a minute, and the letter would fade from existence.

Tim turned and broke into a dead run. He'd jump in his car and go over to Vermillion. With a little luck, Meg would be in her room. He could be holding her in less than fifteen minutes.

When Tim parked his Oldsmobile in front of Carman Hall, the rain had lightened into a gray drizzle. The image of Meg tucked cozily into her dorm room spurred him to action. He stuck Melinda's soggy letter into the glove compartment and slammed his car door shut behind him. He bolted up to the entrance of the girls' dorm, ducking under its blue awning just as another rumble of thunder split the air.

His eyes ran down the list of names on the directory posted outside the door. *Harmon, Hastings, Hidelman, Hill* . . . Tim paused. Where was *Henry*? He looked at the names again, scanning the whole list. There was no Megan Henry.

Tim looked around. The building *was* Carman Hall. And it was definitely the place where he'd dropped off Meg after their date on Saturday. "I must be going blind or something," he muttered. Tim leaned in close to the directory and studied each name. There were eighty names, and twelve of them began with *H*. But there was no Henry.

The front door was locked. He couldn't very well buzz some random girl's room and ask if she knew which room was Meg's. Tim gazed forlornly at the rain. He'd have to go to the pay phone at the Shell station and try to call her. He must be losing his mind.

Suddenly the door flew open and two girls came rushing out. They stopped abruptly when they saw Tim standing, bewildered, under the awning. "Well, hello there," the tall blonde said. "Can we help you with something specific, or are you just hoping to get lucky?" Her friend giggled, and Tim hoped his blushing cheeks didn't show up in the dim light.

"Actually, I'm trying to find Megan Henry. Do you know her?" From the blank look on their faces, Tim figured the answer was no.

Both girls shook their heads. "Never heard of her," the blonde answered. "Are you sure she lives here?"

"I think I'm sure," Tim answered.

The girl who'd been talking to him turned to her friend, who was wearing a big turquoise cowboy hat. "Lorraine, does the name ring a bell?"

"Can't say that it does," Lorraine drawled. "But if I meet her I'll tell her a very wet, very cute guy is conducting a desperate search."

"Thanks. Thanks a lot," Tim said to the girls as they opened their umbrellas and took off down the path, laughing.

Tim decided to let the girls continue on their way before dashing to his car. He wasn't in any mood to give two girls he'd never met before a ride to who knew where.

By the time he'd made it to the car and fastened

his seat belt, Tim had changed his mind about finding Meg that afternoon. The steady rhythm of the ancient windshield wipers was calming his nerves. Wouldn't she think he was some kind of nut, running around in the rain, asking strange girls if they knew where to find her? Getting that letter had really thrown him.

"It's probably a good thing I didn't see her today," Tim said aloud. What had he been planning to say? *Hi, I just got a letter from my ex-girlfriend, and she said she's still in love with me. Want to go out for ice cream?* Tim laughed weakly at the thought. If he'd learned anything from leafing through girls' magazines at Melinda's, it had been this: As soon as a girl smells *rebound,* she's out the door like a shot.

Not that he was on the rebound. Not at all. But Meg still didn't know him that well. And the last thing he wanted was to scare her away by dredging up his bitter past with Mel. He nodded his head resolutely. Some things were better left unsaid. *After all, I wouldn't want Meg telling me something that might make me go ballistic and screw up what's so far the best relationship of my life.*

There was only one solution. He'd worry about the letter another day.

Wednesday night Tim sat next to Meg in Rosedale Library. The textbook he was reading, *Economic and Political Development of Modern Third-World Countries,* was significantly more boring than the sight of Meg's profile. They'd already made one failed attempt at studying. Tim had promised that when they went back into the library he'd make an effort to keep his mind where it belonged—on his third-world development class.

Meg's light green sundress was hitched up over one knee, and the sight of her long, shapely calf was driving him to distraction. He forced his eyes away. He had to at least pretend to concentrate. If he didn't, she'd never want to study at Rosedale again.

He made a show of flipping to the index pages of the thick textbook. As he looked arbitrarily through the pages of names and technical terms, he sneaked a glance at her face. She was still bent over *Gulliver's Travels*, and her eyes appeared to be moving steadily across the page. He sighed.

"I saw that look," Meg whispered. She hadn't moved her head, but he could see her lips moving.

"Sorry," he whispered back. "I was just checking that you're still awake. You're kind of quiet over there."

She let out a soft giggle. "That's because I'm *reading*. Believe it or not, I don't have to sound out the words anymore."

In response, Tim adjusted his position so that his back was facing Meg's side. "This is to prove that I'm not going to peek at you while I'm very doggedly doing my homework," he said. He heard her laugh behind him.

He resumed reading. He couldn't see her, but Tim could still hear Meg's quiet breathing. When he closed his eyes, he imagined that he could even feel her warm breath on the back of his neck. He felt goosebumps developing on his arms, but he was careful not to make a sound.

He flipped to his place in the textbook, finally accepting the fact that he was actually going to have to study with Meg beside him. As he turned the pages a piece of lavender paper caught his eye. Quickly he pulled it out. How had Melinda's letter gotten there? The thing was like a curse.

Then he remembered. He'd picked up the letter right after his Monday seminar on third-world development. Then he'd gone straight to the car. After the bum attempt at finding Meg, he'd taken the letter from his glove box and stuck it in the book. Which he hadn't opened till just then. *Good going, Wilson. Way not to act like a man on the rebound!* Tim stuffed the envelope into the pocket of his backpack and quickly zipped it shut. At the first opportunity, he'd put it someplace safe—like in an incinerator.

The lights in the reading room flashed on and off several times. "What's going on?" Meg asked, glancing up from her novel.

"The library's closing, silly. Don't they do that at Vermillion?" Around them, students were packing up books and noisily shoving around chairs.

"Oh, right. Yeah, they do. I was so absorbed in my reading I didn't realize how late it was." She was still whispering.

"Why are you whispering?" Tim breathed in her ear. He brought his voice up to its normal volume. "No one else is."

Meg's laugh seemed a little shaky. "Just habit, I guess." She closed *Gulliver's Travels* and stood up.

"Let's blow this joint." Meg's eyes were scanning the crowded room. Was she looking for somebody?

Tim took her hand and they sauntered out of the library. Outside, everybody seemed to be talking and laughing extra loudly to make up for the stifling silence of the library.

"Studying together was fun," Meg commented. "If not productive."

"I wish we could see each other more often," Tim said. He steered Meg off the main walkway and plopped down under one of the huge oak trees near the library.

"Yeah. Like every day," Meg answered. She reached up and brushed a stray leaf out of his tangled hair.

"Speaking of every day . . . I went by Carman Hall to see you the other day." There was no need to mention that he'd just received a disturbing letter from his high school sweetheart.

"Oh. Really?" Meg was looking at the ground, poking at an anthill with the end of a small twig.

"Yeah. But I couldn't find your name on the list of residents."

Meg shifted her position. "Oh, didn't I tell you? I switched into Carman in March. I was in Brooks, but my roommate was a real pain. So I left."

Why did she seem to be making a point of avoiding his gaze? It was hard to imagine Meg not getting along with somebody, but maybe her roommate really had been trouble. One thing was clear—she didn't want to talk about it.

"Aha! The mystery is solved. Well, for future reference, what's your room number?" Tim moved so that he could look into Meg's eyes. He was dying to kiss her.

"Oh. Um, room four," she answered.

"Four what?"

"What do you mean, four what?"

"You know, four-A, four-B, four-C . . ."

"Right, right. It's four-A."

"Great. Now I know." Tim leaned in to kiss her.

"But you probably shouldn't come there," she said quickly, just as he was inching forward.

"Why not?" Tim demanded. Meg seemed to have an overdeveloped need for privacy. She never talked about her friends, and when he asked her about her classes, she was usually vague. It was as if she didn't want him to be as big a part of her life as he wanted to be. Maybe he was pushing her too fast.

"Well, guys aren't allowed upstairs. And the downstairs lounge is usually a madhouse. You know, girls in their p.j.'s giggling over stupid magazines and stupider TV shows."

"I guess women's colleges are really different. But what can you do? I'll have to settle for seeing you outside your natural habitat."

Instead of answering, Meg put a cool hand on the back of his neck. Finally he got his kiss. By the time it was over, Tim couldn't remember what they'd been talking about.

Sixteen

"Dude, can I have cuts?" Ollie's voice was urgent and held an edge of conspiracy.

Tim glanced over Ollie's shoulder. There were about forty people behind him in line at the all-you-can-eat cafeteria. Then he looked back at his roommate. "Can you have *cuts?*" he asked.

"Yeah. As in can I cut in front of you in line? From the verb *to cut.* From the Latin root *cutus in linemus.* As in if you don't let me go ahead of you, there's no way I'll get any Mississippi mud cake."

"I wouldn't want to deny you one of the four major food groups. Go ahead." Tim saw a few angry faces glaring at him.

"Thanks, man. You know I'd do the same," Ollie said. He slid his tray onto the metal rack in front of the desserts. Just as the girl behind Tim in line reached for the last piece of plastic-covered chocolate cake, Ollie grabbed it. He flashed her a good-natured grin. "Sorry, ma'am. All's fair in love and food."

Tim groaned and shot the girl an apologetic grimace. She shrugged her shoulders and took a bowl of dried-out peaches. "It's probably for the best," she remarked. "The freshman fifteen can sneak up fast."

Tim laughed. The girl's eyes reminded him of Meg's. They were big and brown. When she smiled, the corners crinkled up, as if she were smiling with her whole face. Then again, the way her red hair curled around her face reminded him a lot of Melinda— only Melinda's hair fell past her shoulders. Tim's head jerked, and he stopped himself. Had he just been thinking about Melinda? He had! He gave himself a couple of quick slaps on the face as he carried his tray over to the juice machine.

"Are you having some kind of spasm, Wilson? Or is self-flagellation a nasty habit you've been hiding from me?" Oliver *would* have to have seen that. Tim couldn't think of a decent response, so he turned and went to search for an empty table in the cavernous dining hall.

Tim shoved two trays of half-eaten food out of the way and sat down at a corner table. A minute later, Ollie moved the trays to the floor and took a seat across from him. Oliver immediately unwrapped his Mississippi mud cake and took a huge bite.

"Are you going to eat dessert first?" Tim asked.

"Sure," Ollie answered, his mouth full of cake. "If I started with fried chicken and carrots, who's to say I wouldn't get full? Then I'd miss out on the good stuff." Ollie scraped off the frosting and licked it from his spoon.

"Aside from the fact that you're making me sick, the simplicity of your life is appealing." Tim cut a precise square of his meat loaf.

"Life is simple. Eat, drink, be merry. That's the golden mantra." Oliver polished off the cake and picked up a drumstick.

Tim sighed. He'd hoped it wouldn't come to this, but he had no choice. He had to ask philosopher-king Oliver Staley for some major advice. "Seeing as you have a detailed understanding of life on this planet, let me ask you a hypothetical question."

"Shoot," Ollie said. He'd already stripped his drumstick of all its meat.

Tim took a deep breath and plunged in. "Let's say you'd just broken up with a girl. Not just any girl. Someone you'd been head over heels for—"

"Is she pretty?" Oliver interrupted.

"A knockout. Anyway, say that just when you'd gotten over this girl, and found someone new—who was really awesome—the first girl writes you a letter telling you she wants to get back together." Tim paused. Ollie seemed to be listening intently. A chicken wing was poised in his fingers.

"Anyway," Tim continued, "what do you think the guy should do about the letter? Should he ignore it? Should he call the girl? Should he tell the new girl everything? What?"

Ollie wiped his mouth with a paper napkin. "Simple," he said. "Call the first girl, but don't mention it to the new one."

"Yeah?" He sounded so sure of himself!

"Sure. Then double your pleasure by dating both of them." Ollie leaned back in his chair and patted his stomach.

"Oliver, that's totally unethical! How can you say that?"

Ollie was laughing hard, and at the same time trying to swallow a mouthful of milk. He made a combination snorting-choking sound. "Chill out, choir boy. I'm joking."

"Ha, ha. You're hilarious. As always, my sides are splitting." Tim gulped down half a glass of orange juice. Of course he shouldn't have counted on his roommate to have a sensitive side.

"You can ditch the hypothetical crap. I saw the letter."

"What letter?" Tim shouted.

"That perfume-soaked piece of purple-passion stationery you got from Melinda. I saw it." Ollie calmly started in on his second dessert, a caramel brownie.

"How did you see it? *Where* did you see it?" Tim demanded.

"In the drawer of your night table. It was in there along with the Wicked Witch of the West's picture and that sappy rose that I assume Meg gave you."

"I can't believe you looked through my stuff."

"What can I say? I was searching for your toenail clippers, and instead I uncovered Tim's Treasure Chest and Souvenir Shop."

Tim moved his tray and put his head down on his hands. "Since you already know my personal business, you could at least help me out. What should I do?"

"Forget you ever got that letter. Shred it. Burn it. Or bronze it, if you want. Just never think about it again."

"Why?" Oliver sounded pretty serious. Tim had a suspicion that Ollie had known all day that this conversation was going to happen.

"Because you've got a good thing going with Meg. Melinda did you wrong. So forget about her. You know what they say—living well is the best revenge."

Tim sat back up and ran his fingers through his hair. "I don't want *revenge*."

"Fine. Great. But if you ask me, answering Melinda's letter will only bring you grief. Even if you just write her and tell her you met somebody else, the fact that you responded will encourage her."

"Hmm . . ." Finally Ollie was making some sense.

"I am assuming correctly that you don't want to get back together with her?"

Tim was silent. He didn't want Mel back . . . did he? He thought of being with Meg at the library the previous night, of their kiss under the tree. He imagined her trusting eyes and the way she made the most casual conversation exciting. No. He didn't want Melinda back.

"Say no more, Ollie. You've convinced me. I'm going to get rid of that letter and forget that Melinda Warren exists. You're looking at a new man." Tim felt better than he had since Monday.

"Glad to hear it," Oliver exclaimed. "Hey, are you going to finish the rest of that lemon meringue pie?"

Tim laughed. When he stopped to think about it, life *was* pretty simple.

•   •   •

The community center parking lot was already half full when Tim arrived at the jazz concert Friday evening. He popped the trunk of the Oldsmobile and pulled out a cooler, a sheet, and his backpack. He surveyed the goods with satisfaction. "One sheet that looks like a picnic blanket, check. Apples, oranges, grapes, check. Chocolate chip cookies, check. Diet soda and mineral water, check. Cheese and crackers, check."

He threw the bedsheet over his shoulder and picked up his backpack and cooler. The cooler bumped against his leg as he picked his way through the crowd gathering on Elysian Field, searching for the perfect spot. The big lawn was full of gently rolling hills and the grass was freshly mowed. It really felt like summer.

Tim spread out his personal version of a gourmet picnic and rested back on his elbows to watch for Meg. On the stage, five musicians sat tuning their instruments and doing sound checks on their microphones. A big banner over their heads read Sonny and the Syncopated Rhythms.

When Tim glimpsed Meg striding across the lawn, her long legs gracefully navigating the growing number of blankets, his breath caught in his throat. She looked so much like a moving sculpture that he almost couldn't register the fact that in minutes she would be beside him, laughing and digging through his backpack for food. He felt a wave of relief that he'd decided to ignore Melinda's letter and keep his past relationship a secret from Meg. Maybe someday, when the time was right, he'd tell her about Melinda. *Like on the night of our fiftieth wedding anniversary, when I know it won't come back to haunt me.*

He considered standing up and waving her over, but watching her was too much fun. Since the night of the wedding reception, when he'd watched her dancing with her father, he hadn't had a chance just to relax and enjoy the way she filled his view. He looked at his watch. Judging from her pace, he'd have her in his arms in about seventy seconds. He sighed happily and did a mental countdown. *Sixty-five, sixty-four, sixty-three . . .*

Meg leaned across the sheet to slice a piece of cheese from the wheel of Brie that sat between them. "It really feels like summer," she commented. The breeze lifted a tendril of her hair and blew it across her face.

"You read my mind," Tim answered. The way she pulled the hair from her mouth made him long to be the unruly strands. "I can't believe we still have a couple of weeks before final exams."

Meg swallowed the rest of her cracker. "And after exams, freedom. A whole summer away from school and tests and rules."

Tim laughed. "Luckily the rules part pretty much ended at high school graduation. Unfortunately, the test part is still alive and well."

Meg cleared her throat. "There's something we haven't talked about before." She paused. "Something important."

Tim's heart raced. Did she know about Melinda? Had someone told her about the letter? If Ollie had said one word, he'd twist off his head and stuff it down—

"Summer," Meg continued, "means that a lot of people—a lot of students, that is—will leave town. They'll go home, or go work at a resort or something."

Tim started breathing again. "That's true. I haven't thought about that for a long time—a certain girl has kept me entirely distracted." He reached over and picked up her hand.

"Well?"

"Well what?"

"What are you doing this summer, Tim? I'll be here. You know, staying at my parents' house and working some dumb job. Where will *you* be? You mentioned the night we met that you'd applied for an internship, but you haven't said anything about it since."

Tim slid closer to Meg so that he could put his head in her lap. Where *would* he be? In January, he and Melinda had sent off resumes to senators and congressmen in Washington, D.C. They'd dreamed of getting internships on Capitol Hill. They'd planned to politick during the day, and at night . . .

"Tim? Are you awake?" Meg's voice brought him back to the present.

He smiled up at her. "Yeah. I'm just thinking about summer. I never heard anything about the internships. I mean, a few congressional assistants wrote back that they'd consider me when the time came, but . . ."

"But so far nothing?"

With Meg running her fingers through his hair,

the topic of summer jobs seemed exceedingly unimportant. Who wanted to go all the way to Washington? If he stayed in town, he could see Meg every night. "So far nothing. And I'm glad. Why should I torture myself by having to wear a suit Monday through Friday, nine to five, when I could stay here and take classes? And maybe I could be a research assistant for one of my professors."

Meg pushed him off her lap and got to her knees. Her face was glowing, and her eyes seemed to be shooting sparks. "Exactly. Why? You can get summer housing—it's supposed to be cheap. And you can earn some cash."

Tim was suddenly excited. "Yeah! I can room with Ollie. He'll be here. And I can start training for the soccer season. It makes perfect sense."

Meg threw her arms around him. "I have a feeling that this is going to be a *great* summer."

He hugged her back, wanting to squeeze her until she melted into his body. "It's going to be the best summer of my life. Correction: *our* lives."

And I won't have to worry about running into Melinda, Tim added to himself. There was plenty of time to worry about the future. Who needed some high-powered job on Capitol Hill? Now was the time to bask in being young and in love. The highest-powered job he could imagine was getting Meg to fall as hard for him as he had fallen for her. *And it's going to be a full-time position*, he thought. *Twenty-four hours a day, seven days a week.*

Seventeen

Not a bad Tuesday afternoon, Tim thought, walking across campus. The sun was shining, the birds were singing, and, best of all, he had a date with Meg that night. He couldn't wait to tell her about his trip to the summer housing office. The place had been crammed with students who'd waited until the last minute to get housing; people had even been shouting at each other over who'd been the first to see a bulletin for open rooms. But the stars had been on his side. The guy manning the desk was a devoted soccer fan. He'd recognized Tim and asked him what kind of room he wanted. "Two-bedroom suite with a fireplace," Tim had told him. "Cheap."

The guy had glanced through a pile of papers on his desk and calmly walked over to the bulletin board. He'd elbowed his way in front of three people and plucked a yellow note off the board. "How does this look, buddy?" the guy had asked.

"Perfect." Tim had grinned at the guy. He'd wanted to hug him, but he'd already been getting mean stares from the still-homeless in front of the board. Tim had looked at them and shrugged. "I called last week," he had lied.

Now he and Ollie had an awesome place to live. As soon as he found a job, his world would be in order. "Birds do it, bees do it . . ." He was in such a good mood that even his own lousy singing voice couldn't bring him down.

Still humming, Tim turned down the path that led to his dorm—and ran smack into a wall of muscle. He took a quick step back and found himself staring at a very startled Rick Honan.

"Rick!" he shouted.

"Tim!" Rick exclaimed at the same time.

They both laughed, and Rick gave him a light punch in the arm. "You'd better watch where you're going, little man. Some dude much bigger than me could take you out."

Tim hadn't seen Rick since the night of his wedding. Since the night he met Meg. It was weird how Rick looked just the same. Except for the gold band on his left ring finger, anyone would think the guy was a young stud instead of an old married man. "Hey, how was the honeymoon?" he asked.

"Sweet as honey, and twice as nice. I give marriage an A plus."

"Those Henry women are something else, huh?"

Rick looked a little taken aback. *Oops*, Tim thought. Maybe Meg hadn't had a chance to tell Rick and Caroline about their relationship yet.

"Don't look at me like I've lost my mind, Honan. I'm talking about Meg."

"Meg?" From the look on Rick's face, Tim knew that Meg definitely hadn't told them yet.

"Yeah. While you and Caroline have been enjoying wedded bliss, I've been seeing Meg. The younger and equally beautiful Henry girl."

"You and Meg?" Rick just stood there. He wasn't exactly smiling, either.

"Yeah. Me and Meg. She's changed my life. I once was lost, and now I'm found. She sends me. All that and more."

"Wow," Rick stammered. "That's something. That's really something."

"Isn't it?" *I hope Meg's not mad at me for spoiling the surprise,* he thought. "I'm seeing her tonight, actually."

"Well, that's great, Tim. Just great. Listen, I'm late to meet Thorton. You know how the coach blows a gasket if he has to wait."

"Don't remind me! I need to go jump in the shower, anyway." Tim turned to continue down the path. "Hey, maybe we could double sometime. You and Caroline, me and Meg."

"Uh, sure. Sounds like fun. I'll have Caroline talk to Meg." Rick sounded puzzled, and his expression was bland.

"Terrific. Catch you later." Tim took off toward his dorm. He hoped Rick didn't think doubling with him and Meg would be boring. Maybe Rick thought they were too young to be much fun.

Well, that was fine with him. As far as Tim was concerned, he was happy to have Meg all to himself.

• • •

Tim reached up to massage his stiff neck. He'd been studying third-world development for almost two hours. Time for a study break. He flipped open his assignment book. It was Wednesday; his test was Friday morning, and he had a track meet Friday night. He'd have to study all night on Thursday, which meant he wasn't going to be able to see Meg until their date Saturday night. So much for the stars being on his side. *There goes schoolwork*, he thought, *rearing its ugly head while I'm trying to have fun*.

He stood up and did a few jumping jacks. He hoped that a little blood circulation would energize him for another few hours of studying. He stopped in midjack when there was a knock at the door. *Uh-oh*, he thought guiltily. It was probably the guy downstairs, coming to complain about the thumping. He jogged over to the door, preparing an apology.

The words fell dead on his lips when he opened the door. The person standing there wasn't his downstairs neighbor. "Melinda!" He couldn't think of anything else to say. "Melinda," he repeated.

She pushed past him and glided into the room. "Surprised to see me?" She was holding a small duffel bag and a few candy roses like the ones he'd brought her on Valentine's Day.

"That's one way of putting it." Tim's heart stopped. The sound of her low, husky voice gave him a shiver.

The last time he'd heard her voice, she'd been whispering to that jerk George on the telephone. He looked at her as if she were a foreign object.

Even viewing her from an emotional vacuum, he had to admit that she looked beautiful. Her auburn hair was piled high on her head, and her faded jeans looked as though they'd been glued on. She was even wearing his favorite shirt: a pale pink smock top with a wide scoop neck.

"Don't roll out the red carpet or anything," she joked. Her voice was confident, but Tim could tell she was nervous. She always chewed the inside of her cheek when she was unsure of herself. She held out the chocolate roses. "Look, I even brought you these."

Melinda wasn't the only one who was nervous. Tim took a few deep breaths. If he let her see the effect she was having on him, Melinda would take the advantage—he'd be at her mercy. If there was ever a time to play it cool, this was it.

"What are you doing here?" Tim didn't make a move toward her. Shaking off the shock of seeing her was hard enough. Acting even pseudo-casual about it would have been mission impossible.

Melinda dropped her duffel bag and the roses on his desk chair and took a seat on the edge of his bed. She pulled out the pins holding up her hair and it came tumbling over her shoulders. "Didn't you get my letter?" she asked.

"Yeah, I got it, but—"

"Well, then, you should be able to answer your own question. *Obviously* I'm here to make up. So let's get started!"

"Started doing what?" He seemed to have lost the ability to form complete sentences. She was wearing bright pink lipstick, and her eyelashes looked like they were about two inches long.

"Started making up, of course." She smiled and fluttered her eyelashes. "Let me give you a hint. Kiss me."

Tim was experiencing a drowning sensation. "Are you crazy? I can't kiss you!"

"Don't tell me you've already forgotten how! It's like riding a bike. Once you learn—"

"Melinda, shut up!" He was trying to stay in control, but things didn't seem to be going well. They didn't seem to be going well at all.

"Come on, Tim. I know you're mad, but we can talk about that later. Now get over here. Please." She'd moved farther onto the bed, and her shoes were now on the floor next to his nightstand.

"Melinda, this isn't a game. You can't just walk in here and expect everything to be fine. In case you forgot, you pulled my still-beating heart out of my chest." Tim felt his pulse racing. Who did she think she was? Had he been such a lovesick puppy that she thought she could just waltz back into his life as if nothing had happened?

Still, it would be so easy to sit down next to her on the bed. He could pull her close and kiss her the way he used to. He still remembered the taste of her lips, the smell of her hair. The months apart hadn't been enough to make him forget.

"I know it's not a game," she said softly. "But think about it. This is one of those truly romantic moments. Two ill-fated lovers have been separated for months. The heroine shows up at her hero's door, ready to reconcile. They take one look at each other and fall into a passionate embrace. . . . You couldn't write a script better than that!"

Tim shoved her duffel onto the floor and gently placed the foil-covered flowers on his desk. When he sat down, he felt as if he were in the electric chair. "Mel . . ."

She walked over to where he was sitting and placed one perfectly manicured hand on his shoulder. Slowly she moved her hand from his shoulder to his face. Her fingers lightly traced the line of his lips. "Don't say anything," she whispered. "Just kiss me."

He brushed her hand away and stood up. *I need to be as far away from her as this shoebox of a room will allow,* he thought. "We need to talk," he said. "Now."

Melinda drew her lips into a thin line and draped herself across his bed. "Fine. If you insist, go ahead and talk."

Getting out the words was harder than he'd imagined. Every time he looked at her face, a different memory resurfaced: the amazing night of their senior prom; the day they'd gotten their college acceptance letters; the entire summer before, when they'd driven aimlessly for hours, not stopping until they felt like pulling over somewhere and . . .

Tim forced the memories away. He had to live in the present, he reminded himself. Melinda wasn't the woman he'd thought she was. Probably she never had been. A thin layer of ice formed around his heart. "I don't know how to say this, so I'll just go ahead and say it."

Her expression had grown dark, and there were tears glistening in her eyes. "Don't," she said softly. "Please don't say it."

Tim gulped. Why did she have to look so vulnerable? So lovable? "I met someone. Not just any-one, but someone I'm really in love with." It was the first time he'd said it aloud. How ironic that he would say those words to Melinda instead of Meg. *I love you, Meg,* he said silently. *I really do.*

Slumped over on his bed, Melinda began sob-bing. Her shoulders shook violently. "No!" she finally shouted. "I don't believe you! You're lying. You're just trying to make me jealous, to get back at me." She stared into his eyes, tears streaming down her face.

"I'm not lying, Melinda. Right now I feel so bad that I almost wish I *were* lying, but I'm not." Against his will, the ice was thawing. He wanted to hate Melinda. He wanted to turn a cold shoulder and kick her out of the room and into the night. But he couldn't.

The line between loving and being in love had been blurred, almost obscured. The realization that he still loved her came as a shock. Months apart hadn't changed the fact that she was beautiful, intelligent, challenging. *But am I in love?* he won-dered. Did he want to forget about Meg and pick up with Melinda where they'd left off in February?

Tim searched Melinda's face for an answer. He tried to imagine the two of them together again, the way it had been in high school. But all his mind would produce were visions of a lonely life without Meg.

Melinda's tears had dried, and when she stood up, her face had the look of steel that he'd seen the night he'd found her with George. "So what's the little tramp's name?" she snapped.

Tim gasped. The window of nostalgia for their lost love slammed shut. "Don't ever say anything like that about Meg!" he yelled. "Who do you think you are? I devoted myself to you for months. But you dated a guy behind my back for weeks and dumped me without so much as an 'I'm sorry,' and now *you're* calling *her* a *tramp?*" He almost wanted to laugh. The situation was spinning wildly out of control.

"So her name's Meg?" At least Melinda seemed to realize that she was in no position to judge him.

"Her name's Megan Henry, and she's wonderful. She's at Vermillion. I'm sure that under different circumstances you'd really like her." *Not that I'll ever give you a chance to find out,* he thought.

"Oh, yeah, I bet we'd be best friends. Maybe the three of us should go out for coffee. Maybe we could do lunch, laugh about old times!" Her voice was rising.

All of a sudden the door opened. "Jeez! It sounds like World War Three in here," Oliver said, walking into the room. When he saw Melinda, he stopped. "Well, well, well, if it isn't the prodigal girl-friend. How cozy."

"Hello to you too, Ollie. I see you're as charming as ever. Crushed any beer cans against your fore-head lately?"

Tim groaned. Even last semester, Ollie and Melinda had been far from forming a mutual admiration society. But at least they'd been civil. "Can you guys hold your fire, please? Remember, we're all adults."

Tim heard Melinda scoff, and Oliver looked at

him as if he were five years old. "Tim, nice guys finish last. You'd better get rid of Her Highness before you-know-who finds out she's here."

Melinda snorted. "Get a life, Oliver."

"At least I'm not chasing old boyfriends halfway down the East Coast."

Tim braced himself for the explosion. Mel didn't take well to insults. He waited, but there was no joke about Oliver's brain being the size of a pea or him being as clean as a gas station bathroom. Instead, Melinda started crying again.

"Hey, Oliver, do you think Melinda and I could be alone for a while? We haven't really had a chance to talk." Melinda sniffled, and her glance at him seemed almost grateful.

Ollie stood for a moment, looking from one to the other. "All right." He sighed. "I'll go stay at Sidney's tonight. But you owe me, roomie. Big time."

Tim nodded. Oliver grabbed a baseball cap and went to the door. "Try not to take it too hard, Melinda. I'm sure you'll find another boyfriend—as the saying goes, there's a sucker born every minute." He laughed and shut the door, just before a pillow came flying at his head. "Missed me!" he taunted from the hallway.

"I really hate that guy," Melinda said unnecessarily.

"He's okay. He's just protective."

Melinda sat back down on his bed. She seemed drained of her fire. "I'll go now. I just didn't want to give Ollie the satisfaction of thinking he'd driven me out." She leaned over to pick up her duffel bag.

Tim took a deep breath. He might end up regretting it for the rest of his life, but there was no way he could let Melinda drive seven hours that night. "Don't be ridiculous. It's late."

"Well, what other option do I have?" She fished in her bag for her car keys.

"Stay here," he answered. He couldn't quite bring himself to look in her eyes.

"Really, Tim? Do you mean it?" she asked, her voice hopeful. For the first time since she'd arrived, she gave him what appeared to be a genuine smile.

"Yes, I really mean I want you to stay here. But I still feel the same."

"Oh." Her face fell.

"You can have my bed, and I'll sleep in Ollie's. I wouldn't want to subject you to his sheets—I don't think they've been washed since the fall."

"You always were a gentleman," she said. She took out her toothbrush and a nightshirt and went into the bathroom. "I'll just be a minute."

While she was gone, the phone rang. Tim looked at his watch. It was probably Meg. Should he pick it up? He thought about Melinda coming out of the bathroom and saying something that Meg could hear over the phone. Meg probably wouldn't understand why he was having another woman stay overnight in his room. After seven rings, the phone was quiet. *I'm sorry, Meg. But it's for the best.*

When he and Melinda had gotten into their separate beds, he reached over and turned out the lights. "Sleep well," he said into the darkness.

He heard sheets rustling, and he glanced over in the general direction of the bed she was sleeping in.

"Tim?" she whispered.

"Yeah?"

"How about a good-night kiss for old times' sake?"

He couldn't deny that he wanted to kiss her. Just one last time, to say good-bye. Without a word, Tim threw his legs over the side of Ollie's bed and stood up. He went to Melinda and placed his lips lightly on hers. She drew him closer for a second, then abruptly let him go.

"I'm sorry it didn't work out, Mel," he said, sliding back into Oliver's bed. "It's kind of tough to imagine that we'll never kiss again."

Melinda laughed quietly. "Never say never, Tim," she said. "Sweet dreams."

Eighteen

Saturday morning Tim was quietly opening and shutting drawers when the sound of Oliver yawning broke the silence. "Good morning," Tim said, pulling a faded yellow T-shirt over his head.

Oliver sat up and stretched. He glanced at the clock. "Where are you off to at ten o'clock in the morning? Didn't anybody ever tell you that Saturday was invented for sleeping till noon?"

"I've got things to do," Tim answered, taking his wallet from the back pocket of the jeans he'd worn home from the track meet the night before.

"You don't have another race today, do you?" Oliver had lain back down in bed. One arm was thrown over his eyes, blocking out the morning sun.

"Nope. I'm going on a little shopping trip."

"*Shopping?* Since when do you go shopping?"

"Since today." Tim counted the money in his wallet and then stuck the wallet in his shorts pocket.

"What's so special about today?"

"Exactly one month ago today I met Meg. It's our anniversary."

"Wilson, you've gone over the edge into cornball land. Nobody celebrates a *one-month anniversary.*"

"Speak for yourself, Ollie. I'm taking Meg to Nabil's tonight, and I want to get her something special."

Oliver chuckled. "And taking Meg out for a fancy night on the town has nothing to do with the fact that Melinda spent the night here on Wednesday?"

"What's that supposed to mean?" Tim walked over to Ollie's bed and hit him over the head with a pillow.

Oliver sat back up, rubbing his eyes. "Sounds like *guilt* to me, buddy-boy."

"Get serious! Why should I feel guilty?"

"Because your ex-girlfriend, whom you've conveniently never mentioned to Meg, showed up at our doorstep and ended up staying the night."

"Ollie, it's not like I *wanted* Melinda to show up out of the blue. I didn't have a choice."

"And I suppose you didn't have a choice when you decided to kiss her?"

"Why did I ever tell you about that? You'd think by now I'd know better."

"Elementary, my dear Watson. You told me for the same reason you're running out to buy Meg a present—guilt."

Tim sighed. Why did Oliver have the annoying habit of letting every thought that went through his brain come out his mouth? "Okay. Maybe I do feel a little guilty. But that has nothing to do with wanting to buy Meg an anniversary present."

"Whatever you say, Wilson. Just do me a favor."

"What?"

"If you ever feel guilty about something you've done to me, keep in mind that I could really use a new Walkman."

"You're a jerk, Oliver," Tim said as he walked out the door.

The streets around the college were fairly deserted. Tim walked from store to store, looking in the window for something that seemed right for Meg. Unfortunately, most of the shops were geared toward the specific needs of student life: eyeglasses, books, towels, vintage clothes, posters, CDs. None of it exactly said *I love you*.

There was an empty lot on Twelfth Street. Most of it was covered with hard brown dirt and an occasional piece of litter. But in the middle of the lot was an old red caboose with a sign over the door that said Harrison's Antiques and Assorted Junk. Tim climbed the three steps to the door and pushed it open. A bell jangled and an old man instantly appeared behind a long glass display case. "Good morning, son. Welcome to Harrison's," he said amicably. "In case you haven't guessed, I'm Harrison."

"Hi there," Tim answered. He looked around the cluttered caboose, his gaze taking in old lamps, heavy wooden trunks, and half-broken rocking chairs. "This is an interesting place."

The man laughed and seemed to follow the path of Tim's eyes around the small store. "I prefer to think of it as magical. I've never had a customer leave without buying some treasure suited perfectly to his or her needs."

Tim smiled, and wandered over to the display case, where a shiny object displayed on a purple velvet cushion instantly caught his eye. "May I look at that?" he asked, pointing to the silver heart.

"Ah, the antique heart necklace. That's one of my more recent acquisitions. I picked it up when I was in New Orleans last week." The man opened the sliding door behind the case and carefully lifted out the necklace.

The heart was about twice the size of a quarter and it hung from a thin silver chain. "It's beautiful," Tim said, turning the heart over in his palm.

"Great gift for a girlfriend, huh?" Harrison sat down on a wooden stool and stuck an ornately carved pipe in the corner of his mouth. "I don't smoke it," he said, gesturing toward the pipe. "I just like chewing on the end."

Tim nodded absently. He was picturing the heart dangling at the base of Meg's long neck. It would set off the hollow of her throat and her well-defined collarbones perfectly. She'd love it.

"I could engrave that for you. Got the tools right here," Harrison added.

Tim looked up. "Really? How much would the engraving cost?"

"For you, I'll do it for free. And I'll give the necklace

a nice polish. I always like to give my first customer of the day a little something extra." He opened a drawer and started taking out some metal tools.

"Thanks! I'll take it." Tim set the necklace on the counter and tried to think of what he wanted to put on the back of the heart. *Happy one-month anniversary?* No, that was too long, and it sounded kind of dry. *Now you have my heart?* Tim shook his head. Too corny. He closed his eyes and envisioned the little heart hanging loosely around Meg's neck. What did it say?

"Figured out what you want me to put on it, son?" Harrison held the heart in one hand and an engraving tool in the other.

Tim opened his eyes. "Yes, Harrison, I know just the words." The buzz of the engraver filled the caboose and Tim gave himself a mental pat on the back. *Now Megan Henry will always know just how important she is to Tim Wilson*, he thought.

As always, Meg was waiting for him at the curb in front of her dorm. He checked the knot of his tie in the rear-view mirror before he jumped out of the Oldsmobile to greet her. "You look even more gorgeous than usual tonight," he said, hugging her close. Meg's short black skirt and red crop top showed off the curves of her body. He breathed in the scent of her hair and neck. "And you smell delicious."

Meg gave him a soft kiss on the cheek. "I put a little vanilla behind my ears," she giggled. "It's a well-known aphrodisiac."

"I think it's working!" He kissed her tenderly on the lips before opening the car door. "It's a good thing you didn't shower in it. I might not have been able to control myself."

They held hands as Tim drove to Nabil's. It was already dark out, and the streetlights cast a soft light over Meg's face. She looked so serene and trusting that he was tempted to blurt out the whole story of Melinda paying him an unexpected visit. *Maybe later*, he thought. *I want to make sure the mood tonight is just right.*

"You look pensive," she said suddenly. "Like you're trying to think of a way to achieve world peace or something."

They had stopped for a red light. Tim put the car in park and turned away from the steering wheel. "I'm just thinking about how much I want to kiss you again," he said, leaning close to her. "Want to kill twenty seconds before the light turns green?"

She nodded silently and traced the line of his left eyebrow with her index finger. He felt a familiar tingle at the back of his neck as he closed the space between them. Tim didn't pull away from their kiss until the driver behind them blared his horn.

"Whoops," Meg said. "We'd better not do that again!"

"It must be the vanilla," Tim answered, joining the traffic.

Once they'd arrived at Nabil's and been seated, Tim tried to broach the dreaded Melinda topic. "Meg, I've been wanting to tell you something for a while now, but the time's never been right—"

His words ended abruptly when the waiter came

up with their menus. *Oh, well,* he thought. At least he'd tried.

While they ate their entrees, Tim told her about the progress in his summer plans. "Ollie and I signed the housing form today. As of June second, we'll be official residents of Lakesmith Hall."

"It sounds great," Meg said. "It's too bad you didn't have that wood-burning fireplace last winter instead of this summer, when it'll be a hundred degrees and humid every day."

"You're telling me! But we're hoping we might be able to swing staying on through the school year."

"When am I going to meet the infamous Oliver Staley, anyway? I feel like I already know him."

"I could ask you the same thing. I'm starting to think that your roommate, Gretchen, is just an imaginary friend." He chewed silently on his last bite of filet mignon. "You know, we should introduce them. Maybe we could do some successful matchmaking. Ollie's a really great guy when you get to know him."

Meg seemed to be choking on her grilled prawns. She took a huge gulp of mineral water and coughed into her napkin.

"Are you okay?" Tim asked anxiously. "Do you want me to thump you on the back?"

She shook her head vigorously and took another sip of water. "Sorry. I'm fine now." She cleared her throat. "I, uh, guess some of my prawn went down the wrong way." A waiter appeared to take away their empty dishes, and Meg sat back in her chair. She looked a little pale.

Tim patted the inside pocket of his linen jacket. He felt the shape of the small box against his chest.

He breathed deeply, not quite sure what he wanted to say to Meg. *I'll just give it to her,* he decided. The engraving said it all. He pulled the box out of his pocket and put it between them on the table.

"Happy one-month anniversary, Meg," he said.

She reached out and put her hand on top of his. "You didn't have to give me anything!" she exclaimed, squeezing his hand a little.

"I wanted to. It's sort of an old-fashioned token saying that we're going steady." Tim groaned silently. Could he sound more like an idiot? He wished he'd stuck to his original plan and kept his mouth shut. Meg probably thought he was the biggest sap on earth.

She looked at him with a hint of a smile. It looked like there were tears in her eyes. *Must be the candlelight,* he told himself. "Open it," he prompted, pushing the box closer to her side of the table.

She untied the silk bow and lifted the pale blue lid of the box. When her eyes fell on the heart, she gasped. *I'll have to go back to the caboose and thank Harrison,* Tim thought. His elegant wrapping had added an extra touch of elegance to the antique necklace.

"Turn it over," Tim said. He knew his expression was serious, but inside he was grinning from ear to ear. *How's that for a cornball, Ollie?* he silently asked his roommate.

"'M.—Love always—T.,'" she read. She was staring at the words, but she didn't look as happy as he'd expected. He'd wanted her whole name engraved on the heart, especially since she had the same first initial as Melinda, but Harrison had said there wasn't room.

After thinking for a few moments, he'd shrugged and told the old man to go ahead with the *M*. It wasn't as if Melinda would ever see the necklace anyway.

Meg's eyes had clouded over and she looked kind of sad. Maybe even irritated. "I don't know what to say," she finally said.

You're being paranoid, Wilson, he scolded himself. She was just a little overwhelmed. "Say you'll wear it," he said softly.

Meg seemed to hesitate before answering. Tim's heart dropped. Did she think the necklace was stupid? Even worse, did she know something about Melinda? Maybe she'd been waiting for a chance to spring it on him. And if she did know, did she think he'd originally gotten the necklace for his ex-girlfriend? The idea was too awful to consider.

"Of course I'll wear it," she whispered. She held out the necklace, and Tim walked around the table so he could fasten it around her neck. It looked perfect—just as he'd imagined.

As Tim went back to his chair he felt as if his feet weren't even touching the ground. But a few minutes later, his heart was aching dully. Meg wanted to go home. Why? She had seemed fine earlier, and now all of a sudden she had a splitting headache? Tim bit his lip as he paid the check. When he'd suggested she go out to the parking lot ahead of him, she'd stood up so fast her chair had almost tipped over. She'd run out of the restaurant with her head down, almost as if she were trying to avoid someone. But that was ridiculous. . . .

There was only one explanation for her behavior. *She doesn't want to commit. She feels like my*

giving her the heart is a trap. She wants to be free.
It was all painfully familiar. Were all girls alike, just
out for a good time?

When he got into the car, where Meg was waiting, she slid over on the seat. They were almost
touching, but she was massaging her temples with
both hands. He couldn't think of anything to say,
and they drove toward her dorm in a dead silence.

Their good-bye was like something out of a night-
mare. It was the opposite of what he'd anticipated
earlier in the day. Instead of a long and passionate
kiss, they shared a cold embrace. Meg scurried away
without giving him even a parting glance. As Tim
drove in the direction of the university, the streets
seemed to have an eerie, abandoned quality. His
own head had started to pound with unanswered
questions. He couldn't really believe that Meg didn't
love him. The chemistry between them was too
right. She couldn't have been just pretending to care
about him all these weeks. It was almost as if she
was *scared* of something. Seeing the necklace
seemed to have triggered some unexplainable nega-
tive vibes. *Either she knows the truth about Melinda
and for some reason hasn't said anything about it,
or— Or what?* A new possibility entered his head.
Maybe she'd been hurt in the past, too. And maybe
the guy had given her a necklace or some other piece
of jewelry at one point. Maybe she associated gifts
like that with the jerk who had broken her heart.

Tim wanted to embrace the idea. It explained
everything and left plenty of room for a future
between him and Meg. He clenched his fists
around the steering wheel, thinking about some

guy treating Meg badly. *She probably didn't want to tell me about him for the same reason that I didn't want to tell her about Melinda.*

The closer Tim got to campus, the more convinced he was that his theory was right. By the time he walked into his room, he almost felt okay. He had pulled off his tie and undone the top button of his white oxford-cloth shirt. "Hey," he said to Ollie, who was listening to an old heavy-metal CD and playing air guitar.

Oliver turned off the stereo immediately and looked at Tim with a wary expression. "What happened tonight, man? Meg just called and asked me to tell you that she's sorry and that she returns the sentiments on the necklace. Whatever *that* means."

Tim sat down on his bed to untie his tight dress shoes. "We had kind of a weird night—I don't want to talk about it."

Instead of slinging some biting remark at him, Ollie tapped his head thoughtfully. "You know what you need, Wilson?"

Tim laughed bitterly. "If I knew that, you think I'd be sitting here like a lost puppy?"

Ollie went on as if he hadn't heard him. "You need a night out with the boys. Throw on some jeans and come over to the Beta house with me."

"No way. I'm just going to sit here and listen to some jazz."

"Give me a break," Ollie shouted. "I've made up my mind. You're going out with me, and you're going to lighten up."

Tim turned the idea over in his mind. He *did* need to lighten up. And he'd barely seen Ollie outside of their room since he'd been dating Meg. "All right, already, I'll go."

Ollie gave him a high-five and threw him the keys to their room. "Watch out, world, Staley and Wilson are together again," he shouted. "Just wait, man. Tonight will be great."

Tim looked longingly at the phone before he shut the door behind him. "Sure," he muttered. "We'll have a real blast."

Nineteen

"Maybe I should try studying at the library," Tim muttered Friday night. He'd been trying to keep Meg off his mind for the last few hours, but it was impossible. He hadn't seen her for almost a week, and he had over twelve more hours to go. Even though they'd talked on the phone every day since their awkward parting after dinner at Nabil's, they hadn't been able to find time to see each other. It was like the cosmic force that had brought them together was suddenly struggling to keep them apart. And until he kissed her again, nothing was going to feel right.

Tim jumped when the phone rang. *That's her*, he thought. He could sense it. Maybe she'd gotten her paper finished and could go out that night after all. He grabbed the receiver on the second ring, his heart pounding. "Hello?" he said breathlessly. *How embarrassing. It must sound like I've been doing laps around my bed.*

"Hi, Tim. Do you still recognize my voice, or should I tell you who's calling?" Melinda's tone was icy and formal.

A knot formed in his stomach. His bad day had suddenly become significantly worse. *Please let this be a bad dream.* He pinched himself. *Damn!* he thought. *No such luck.*

"Melinda. Hello." He didn't know what to say next. "How's it going?" didn't really seem appropriate.

"Not the friendliest greeting I've ever gotten, but at least you didn't hang up on me." Was that amusement he detected in her voice?

"You know I'd never do that." He paced back and forth, twisting the phone cord around his fingers.

"No, I guess you wouldn't." There was a pause. "Tim, I can practically hear you pacing. Why don't you sit down for a minute?"

He stopped pacing and leaned against his desk. "Okay, I'm sitting." He could tell from the casual way she was talking that she had something to say. She was purposely trying to make him nervous.

"So, how's your girlfriend?" The condescension in her voice was making his blood boil.

"Her name is Meg. And she's fine."

"Oh, I know her name's Meg. I know lots of stuff about her."

Tim could feel the pulse in his neck beating frantically. Melinda was up to something, and he had a bad feeling that he was about to find out what it was.

"Don't play games, Mel. If you want to tell me something, go ahead."

"I'm not the one who's playing games. That's probably more up your girlfriend's alley. I bet she likes playing hopscotch, and Barbie, and Go Fish. . . ."

The last bit of his patience ran out. If Melinda hadn't gotten the message that things were completely finished between them, he was going to make sure it came through loud and clear right that second. "Shut up. Just shut up. I don't know what the hell you're trying to accomplish, and I don't want to know. I'm going to hang up now—"

"Wait!" she shouted.

"Okay. Tell me what you want to tell me and *then* I'm going to hang up."

"Fine, I will." There was a long pause, and Tim wasn't sure she actually had anything to say. "Did you know your girlfriend is only fifteen years old?"

All of the blood in Tim's body was rushing to his head. "What?" he yelled. "You're lying! What do you think you're doing?"

Melinda's laughter was low and husky. "I'm not lying, Tim. Megan Henry is not in college. She's a sophomore at Southwest High School. She lives with her parents. You can check it out for yourself. It's all true."

There was something dangerously calm about the way Melinda was delivering this information. It was as if she knew he was trapped in a corner, and she wanted to watch him squirm. But it had to be a trick. Meg couldn't be fifteen! She went to Vermillion. She was a freshman, just like him. She was taking French, and Literature 101, and Introduction to

World History. She was planning to be an English major. All of the details about Meg's life that he'd learned were rushing through his brain.

"Get a grip, Mel. You had me going for a second there, but I know you're lying. I don't know why, but that can be your own little secret. I've gotta go." He wanted to hang up the phone, but some part of his subconscious wouldn't let him do it.

"Well, I guess I wasn't being *totally* honest," Melinda corrected herself. "She's really sixteen. As of today, that is. It's her birthday."

Tim was engulfed by a drowning sensation. His head felt light, and he found himself sitting on the floor, his knees bent under his chin. "Today is not, I repeat, not Meg's birthday. Right now she's in her room working on a paper. For English. It's on *Gulliver's Travels.*"

"Wow, she really thinks of everything, doesn't she? She's probably fabricated stories about everything under the sun: a fake roommate, a fake favorite professor, a fake advisor. I guess that makes you her fake boyfriend." The cruelty in Melinda's voice was beyond anything he would have expected from her. The thought that he'd actually cared about her for so long made his flesh crawl.

"Even if you were telling the truth, which you're obviously not, how would you know this stuff? It's not possible."

"I was wondering when we were going to get around to that question. I must say, I'm pretty proud of my own detective work. It's a long story. Where should I start?"

"Just *tell* me." He could hear how desperate his voice sounded. Mel probably could, too.

"After I left your dorm that morning, I really wanted to see a picture of Meg. I don't why. I guess I wanted to see the girl I'd lost out to. So I went to the registrar's office and asked to look at the freshman face book. There was no Megan Henry."

Tim breathed again. "That's because Meg doesn't go to school here! I think I told you that." He felt his vision returning.

"Let me finish, Tim." When he didn't say anything, she continued. "When I was standing there, I remembered you'd said something about Vermillion. So I put two and two together and got directions to go over there."

"So?"

"I looked at their freshman face book, too. No Megan Henry."

Tim let out an impatient sigh. "Melinda, lots of people aren't in the face book. Ollie, for instance."

Melinda went on as if he hadn't said anything. "I decided to make one last attempt to find a picture of her at the university. After all, I wasn't positive that she supposedly went to Vermillion. Anyway, when I went back to the registrar's, a girl in the office overheard me asking about how I might find a picture of a student." She paused.

"Yeah? Go on."

"The girl told me she might know whomever it was I was looking for, so I told her it was Megan Henry. To make a long story short, this girl—her name's Laura or Laurie or something—told me that Caroline Henry had gone to the university."

The name Laurie had made Tim's stomach tighten up again. Could it just be a coincidence? Lots of girls had that name. "Just get to the point," he commanded.

"I *was* getting to the point. Laurie told me that she knew Meg Henry. But she said Meg went to high school, not the university. From there, it all started clicking. I did some very simple research, asked a few questions, and *voilà.*"

"I still don't believe you," Tim said firmly.

"Suit yourself. Just don't come crying to me when someone calls you a cradle robber."

He couldn't take it anymore. Tim slammed down the phone and punched his fist into the wall. Then he sat down at his desk and put his head in his arms. He thought about every day of the last five weeks. The wedding. His first conversation with Meg. He remembered how he'd gone to Carman Hall looking for her the day he'd gotten that letter from Melinda. Finally he tried to replay in his mind what Tina Wollman had said to him at the track meet. She'd said something about not knowing a girl like Meg was his style. She'd also said something about Meg being a sophomore, and he had corrected her, saying Meg was a freshman. After that she'd shrugged her shoulders and said, "Different strokes."

A sophomore. The words echoed in his mind. Had Tina meant Meg was a tenth grader? Against his will, a thousand inconsistencies raced through his mind. Meg waiting at the curb. The way she never wanted to stay out very late. And just the other day, Rick had seemed so surprised that he was dating

Meg. The pieces came flying together like some twisted jigsaw puzzle. His whole body ached, and his head felt as if it would explode. "It's true," he said aloud. "Meg's been lying to me since the start."

He thought saying the words would make him feel better. Or at least more in control. Instead, he felt the air around him closing in like a suffocating blanket. He tried to think of any excuse, no matter how implausible, that would make what Melinda had told him untrue. But his mind was blank.

He could see Meg's laughing face. He could feel her soft, full lips against his. The images cut through him like a sharp knife. Tim forced himself to stand up. When he looked around the room, everything in it seemed strangely out of focus. He heaved himself face down onto his bed. For the first time since the night he'd lost Melinda, hot tears streamed down his face. He lay there sobbing, silently cursing himself for having fallen prey to another woman. *Girl*, he amended bitterly.

He didn't know how long he lay there crying. When he heard Oliver's key turn in the lock, Tim quickly threw himself under the covers and turned his face toward the wall. By the time Ollie got into the room, Tim had closed his eyes and steadied his breathing. As far as he was concerned, he was asleep. Permanently.

Saturday morning Tim jogged slowly to the park where he was supposed to meet Meg. His mouth was dry, and his head felt as if it were filled with cotton. When he'd woken up, it had taken a couple of seconds for him to remember why he had such a sick feeling in the pit of his stomach. When Melinda's phone call came back to him, he'd had to suppress the urge to scream and bang his head against the wall.

But out in the sunshine, looking at a happy couple with a baby stroller, he allowed himself a glimmer of hope. Maybe it was all okay. Maybe there was some rational explanation, and he was just too dense to figure out what it was. He couldn't help the familiar sense of expectation that always accompanied him on his way to see Meg. Despite everything, he couldn't wait to hug her and kiss her. When she was next to him, living and breathing, he might realize that the whole notion of her being a high school kid was absurd.

But what if it wasn't absurd? What if all his doubts were solidified when he saw her? Should he confront her on the spot? Should he demand an explanation? If she denied it, he'd have to tell her about Melinda's phone call. Unless he was willing to lie outright, he'd have to confess that his ex-girlfriend had been playing private investigator. And what if he told her that, and it turned out that Meg had been telling the truth all along? She'd probably hate him. She'd think he still talked to Melinda all the time. She might even think he'd been cheating on her.

The endless round of questions circled through his mind like a fast-spinning wheel. There was no way to second-guess the situation.

He was still panting from the exertion of his jog when he saw Meg walking toward him. Her face brightened when he waved, and she ran the last few steps.

He followed his first impulse and gripped her in a tight hug.

"I've missed you," she said.

His heart melted. She felt so good in his arms that he simply wanted to block everything else out of his mind. *I'll just let myself act normally for a while,* he decided. *If I don't get uptight, the answers will come to me.* "I've missed you, too," he said. The unexpected passion in his voice was almost frightening.

As they walked toward the park's playground the muscles in his jaw unclenched. It almost seemed like a regular Saturday. The carefree atmosphere of the park was catching, and Tim reached for Meg's hand.

Then, out of nowhere, two girls came charging up the path straight toward them. "Meg, wait!" one of them called.

Meg pulled her hand from his and slowed down. As she stopped in front of the girls she seemed to be avoiding his eyes. "Hi, Alana. Hi, Felicia."

Tim glanced back and forth at the two girls. One of them had braces on her teeth, and the other looked like she hadn't even hit puberty; obviously they weren't from Vermillion. *Slow down,* Tim told himself. Meg was from town. Maybe she'd babysat one of the girls when she was younger.

"Happy late birthday," the girl with braces said. "You're so lucky you can drive now!"

The girl continued talking, but Tim didn't hear a word she said. He felt paralyzed. His last flicker of hope sputtered and died. It was over.

"Tim!" Meg was shouting at him. "Tim, please, listen to me."

He didn't respond immediately. The girls were walking quickly in the other direction, and Meg was looking at him with tears in her eyes. "I was going to tell you—"

He started shouting. He didn't even know what he was saying, except that it was cruel. Everyone else in the park faded into the background. He didn't care if they heard him; he was far beyond rational thought. *Just like Melinda,* he cried to himself. *She lied to me.* What an idiot he was. He loved Meg; he'd overcome his fear of letting himself become vulnerable to another person, but it had all been for nothing. Now he was even worse off than he'd been the night of Valentine's Day.

He sat down on the top of a picnic table and looked at Meg. He felt as if he was seeing a stranger. "You're sixteen," he said. "From the first night, you've been lying. Have you and your friends been having a good laugh about this? Ha, ha, the poor sucker eats up everything Meg says." He had to choke out the words. His throat felt swollen and he could barely breathe.

"No! Tim, I swear, it wasn't like that. I love you! I've just been scared. . . ." Her voice trailed off, and she wiped tears from her pale cheeks.

"Scared? *Scared?* How do you think I feel?" The world was spinning crazily around him.

"If you want to hate me, I understand."

The sadness in her voice made Tim's heart ache even more. This time when he looked in her eyes, he saw the Meg he knew. The Meg he loved. His shoulders sagged; he was exhausted. "I don't hate you, Meg. I still—" He wouldn't let himself finish the sentence. He couldn't say those words.

"You still love me?" she whispered, touching him lightly.

The sensation of her hand on his knee was too much to bear. He shook his head miserably. "I don't know what I feel," he said. He had to get out of that park. He needed to get away from the blue sky, the chirping birds, the sound of laughter. "I need to be alone for a while," he said quietly.

He hopped off the table and took off down the path. Later, he'd make sense of what had happened. Right then he needed to run. He needed to sweat out the tears and the anger. "Call me!" he heard her shout after him.

He didn't look back. He shrugged his shoulders and picked up his pace. *Good-bye, Meg,* he said silently. *I really loved you.*

Twenty

The letter from Washington, D.C., was sitting on his desk when he got back to the dorm. Ollie had put a note on top of it: *Certified mail! Looks like good news. Won't it be a riot to tell your senator that you'd rather be coaching Little League?* Tim stuffed Oliver's note in the bottom of the trash can and opened the letter.

Dear Mr. Wilson:

We're happy to inform you that you've been selected out of a large pool of applicants to be one of Senator Higgins's two summer interns. We'll arrange housing within the next week. Please call us at your earliest convenience. . . .

He didn't need to stop and think about the offer. Tim studied the phone number on the letterhead and dialed it quickly. The office was closed, but he left a concise message on the answering machine. When he set the receiver down, he felt calmer. "I'm going to D.C.," he said aloud. "I'm going to work on Capitol Hill." It was something he'd always wanted to do, but he couldn't muster any excitement. The job was simply the most expedient way to get far away from Meg. Far away from the whole past year, really.

Something occurred to him. *What if Mel got an internship, too?* In a flash, he realized that he didn't care if she had. Breaking up with Meg didn't change the fact that whatever had once existed between him and Melinda had been over for a long time.

He took a deep breath and steeled himself for the next couple of weeks. He had exams to study for. He had to get ready for his last track meet. At some point he'd have to tell Ollie some version of what had happened. And whether he liked it or not, he was going to be thinking about Meg. A lot.

Winthrop Lane was dark and quiet. Tim drove slowly down the street looking for number seventy-six.

It had been over a week since he'd heard from Meg. Whenever the phone rang, his heart pounded. Exams had been the focus of his existence, and he'd thrown himself into making up for the slacking off he'd done over the past few weeks.

When he saw the pretty white house, Tim pulled his Oldsmobile over to the other side of the street and switched off his headlights. *There it is,* he thought. *This is where Meg would go after I dropped her off at Carman Hall.* It had been easy to find her real address. As soon as he'd opened the white pages to the *H*'s, his eyes had been drawn to the small type: *76 Winthrop Lane.*

It was late Monday night, and there was only one light shining in the house. He could see that the window was open; a curtain fluttered gently in the breeze. *That must be Meg's room,* he realized. She was probably sitting in her room at that moment—maybe she was even thinking about him.

He wanted more than anything to ring the doorbell. He wanted to see the place where she lived, to talk to her parents. He wondered vaguely if she had a dog. But he sat motionless in the car, staring at the square of light on the second floor. After about fifteen minutes, he put the car in gear and pulled away from the curb. Meg's house wasn't open to him. He'd never been invited into that private, secret world.

He'd find her the next day. *I can't leave without seeing her face just one more time.*

He'd probably driven past Southwest High a hundred times during the past year. *But I never thought I'd actually go in,* he said to himself. Especially not to see the girl he was in love with.

He stood in the large parking lot, waiting for Meg to come out of the school building. If she was surrounded by giggling friends, he'd hop back in his car and take off. The last thing he wanted was to be an object of curiosity for a bunch of nosy sixteen-year-old girls.

His heart skipped a beat when he saw her walk through the door and down Southwest's front steps. She strolled across the front lawn, her head down and a notebook swinging loosely in her hand. She gave a short wave to a girl sitting nearby on the grass, and continued her slow gait. Tim stared at her as she got closer; she hadn't seen him yet, but from the pounding of his heart he knew that the moment of recognition was only seconds away.

When she saw him, her eyes widened. She hurried toward him, staring. Her smile was tentative, almost shy. "Hi," she said. He was torn between wanting to punch her in the nose and wanting to grab her and kiss the breath out of her. He did neither.

They walked over to the bleachers next to the football field and climbed to the top. She was sitting so close that he could feel the heat from her body. "I got the internship with Senator Higgins," he finally said.

Her face flushed. "But you're staying here," she said, her voice trembling. "You're going to take a class and coach Little League and—" She stopped. Her hands gripped the edge of the bleachers tightly.

"The letter from Washington was a sign, Meg. A lot of stuff has happened to me this year. Not just with you, either. I haven't told you everything about me . . . but I guess there's not really any point to it now." He fell silent. When she didn't say anything, he continued. "I need to escape."

When she spoke, her voice was barely a whisper. "So I won't see you?"

It took all of his willpower to answer her. He wanted to take back everything he'd said. If only they could turn back the clock to the night they'd met and start over. "No."

She tried to change his mind. He could hear the pain in her voice. *At least she really does love me,* he thought. *She's as big a wreck over this as I am.* But he couldn't just kiss and make up. If he stayed in town and tried to work things out between them, he'd end up resenting her. He knew from experience that betrayal wasn't the kind of thing that disappeared overnight.

And he still had a lot of emotional baggage from his breakup with Melinda. He hadn't thought so earlier that spring, but the past week had been proof that he'd been wrong. He'd spent the past few days thinking about both of them, wondering why they'd needed to hurt him so badly. As hard as he tried, he couldn't separate their actions. The only difference was that he was still in love with one of them. When he went to sleep, he dreamed of holding Meg in his arms. When he was in the shower or studying in the library, he'd laugh out loud remembering funny things that she'd said.

Maybe someday he would be able to put this in the past. If Meg was willing to wait for him, anything was possible. "Nothing's written in stone," he said in a low voice. "Maybe when you're older . . ."

He could tell from the expression on her face that

she thought he was feeding her a line. She seemed closed off, as if they had already said their last good-bye. "Someday," she echoed hollowly. "Sure."

They both seemed to know that the conversation was over. Any have-a-nice-summer small talk would have been twisting the knife in both their hearts. Tim wiped his eyes and made a valiant attempt at a smile.

"How about a kiss good-bye?" he asked. When Meg nodded, he took her in his arms one last time.

He could taste the salt from her tears on her lips. And her fingers were shaking when she raked them through his hair. Tim's breath shuddered as he pulled her into a bear hug. He put his face against her neck and breathed in the familiar scent of her shampoo. After a long time, he pushed her gently away from him. With his thumb, he brushed away the tears that trickled down her cheeks. Then he touched the silver heart she wore around her neck. "Give me a minute to get to my car and drive away," he whispered.

He couldn't bring himself to say good-bye, so he turned and started down the bleachers. Walking away from her felt like a funeral march.

Driving out of the parking lot, he said the words that had been hovering on his lips for the past week: "M.—Love always—T."

Rick opened the front door before Tim had a chance to ring the bell. "I saw your car," he explained. "Come on in."

When he walked into the living room, the first

thing Tim noticed was Meg's collage hanging over the fireplace. Fascinated, he stared at the many pictures. Most of them were of Rick and Caroline, but Meg had included a few of her and her cousin when they were younger. In the photographs, Meg's face was bright and smiling; it was hard to imagine that she was the same girl he'd shared a bittersweet kiss with the day before.

Rick gestured for Tim to sit down on the sofa. "I heard about your internship," he said "Congratulations."

Tim gulped. "Uh, thanks, but to be honest, I didn't come to talk about that."

Rick smiled. "I figured as much."

"Rick, I'm sorry about everything that happened with Meg. I honestly didn't know she was only fif-teen—"

Rick held up his hand. "Hey, it's Caroline and I who should be apologizing to you. We've known for a while that Meg was lying to you, but we didn't know what to do about it. She seemed so in love. It would have broken her heart if we'd gone behind her back and revealed her secret."

Tim nodded. "I'm glad to hear you say that. The part about her really loving me, I mean. It's been difficult to know what the truth is lately." He bit his lip, his eyes still on the colorful collage.

Caroline appeared suddenly at the doorway to the living room. "I couldn't help overhearing," she said, crossing the room. She propped herself on the arm of the sofa, draping one arm casually around Rick's shoulders. "Tim, I don't know if any-body really understands the truth about love. But one thing is for sure—it can make a normally sane, rational person do some crazy things."

Tim nodded mutely. He pictured himself driving up to Melinda's college in a snowstorm. Then he remembered how he'd parked in front of Meg's house, for no reason at all, in the dead of night.

"Try not to judge her too harshly, Tim. The worst punishment she's gotten is knowing that she hurt you. You've got to believe that."

Tim stood up. "Thanks, Caroline. I do. When you see Meg, will you tell her I'm not mad anymore? I just need to spend some time in a new place, away from everything."

"Of course I'll tell her," Caroline answered.

Rick walked him to the door. He gave Tim's shoulder a quick squeeze. "I hope you come back next year, buddy. The soccer team really needs you."

"I'll keep that in mind." Tim walked down the front steps and out to his car. *So long, Rick,* he said silently. *Thanks for inviting me to your wedding and giving me a chance to fall in love.*

The small plane picked up speed as it taxied down the runway. Tim tightened his seat belt and leaned his head back against the pillow that the flight attendant had given him. He closed his eyes and mulled over the conversation he'd had with Ollie on the way to the tiny airport.

"Summer's not going to be the same without you, Wilson," Oliver had commented.

"It'll probably be better," Tim had answered. "Now you've got your own car." He'd decided to let Ollie keep the Oldsmobile for the summer. The guy in Senator Higgins's office had said he could walk to work in D.C., and he'd heard that finding parking spaces in the city would be a pain. Besides, he'd gone through some rough times in the Olds. He was ready to let it go for a while.

"I must say, driving this baby does feel good. And it's a perfect make-out spot for all the chicks I'm going to meet while I'm lifeguarding."

"You'll never change," Tim had said with a laugh. Speeding down the highway, he had felt almost lighthearted.

"Would you really want me to?" For once, Oliver's voice had sounded serious.

"Nah, I guess not. Somebody has to be obnoxious and cynical."

"I wouldn't want you to change, either, roomie. I think your hopelessly romantic soul does me good."

Tim had looked out the car window and frowned. "Well, I'm glad it's doing *somebody* good. It sure hasn't worked for me."

"You shouldn't give up on Meg so easily. Unlike the Wicked Witch of the West, I have a feeling that you and Megan Henry haven't seen the last of each other."

"How could you know that? You've never even met her!"

"Don't need to. I told you, I have a feeling."

"Well, you're wrong. Meg and I are history."

Tim opened his eyes. He'd always loved the sensation of being in a plane when it lifted off the ground. A rush of adrenaline surged through his veins as he looked at the town receding fast below him.

He pressed his fingertips against the thick plastic window. The town had come to mean a lot to him over the past year. He and Ollie had started out hating each other and then become best friends in that town. He'd finished his first year of college and been the star of both the soccer and the track teams. Most of all, he had fallen out of and then back into love there. If he transferred to Georgetown, could that university ever be as important to him?

He laughed at himself. If he'd learned anything, it was not to try to predict the future. He'd take one day at a time and see what happened. *And from now on,* he thought, *I'm going to be completely honest. With everybody—including myself.*

There was a beautiful sunset over Washington, D.C. Tim sighed and walked away from the big bay window that took up half of one of the walls of his rented room. He picked up the picture he'd been looking at earlier and rested against the pillows on his bed. He'd been in D.C for nearly two months now and he still had to fight with himself constantly to stop from dwelling on thoughts of Megan Henry.

He'd taken that photo out of its drawer at least fifty times during the last several weeks. It was the only one he had of Meg—they'd had it taken that night at Sam's Big World of Fun, right after their ride on the Ferris wheel. He hugged the picture to his chest, remembering the way Meg had laughed and teased him when he'd insisted they go into the tiny photo booth.

His laughter subsided when a light knock on the door startled him. He quickly stuck the picture between the pages of a book and went to open the door. *Probably the landlady,* he guessed. Maybe she'd gotten someone to fix that leak in the shower.

He opened the door and took an involuntary step backward. She was standing right in front of him, wearing jean shorts and a white tank top. Her hair was tied back in a loose ponytail. After a few seconds, he managed to get himself together enough to say her name out loud.

"Meg."

"Hi there," she said. She stood just outside the door, shifting from one foot to the other. The silver heart necklace shone brightly against the white of her top.

He reached out and touched her face. "It's really you," he breathed.

She laughed softly and took a tiny step forward. "In the flesh." Her smile was questioning, but her eyes were warm and open.

He took her outstretched hand and pulled her inside the spacious room. "I've never been so happy to see anybody in my whole life!" Until the words were out, he hadn't even realized how true they were.

"I'm so glad you said that," she said with a laugh.

Tim pulled her toward him. He ran one finger down the side of her cheek. Meg's skin was even softer than he'd remembered. She stepped closer still, and the fresh smell of summer filled his senses. She was everything he'd been dreaming about for the last few weeks, and more. They pressed their bodies together, and when their lips met, Tim felt his whole body heat up. He tried to communicate all his feelings of love and longing in that one searing kiss.

Meg pulled away slightly, but she kept his hand clasped in hers. "We have a lot to talk about," she said.

"Yeah. There's so much I need to tell you. I've picked up the phone to call you so many times. . . ."

She nodded. "Me too."

"I know you're young. Really young. But I can't help the way I feel. I love you." He held his breath, waiting for her response.

"I know I've still got a lot of growing up to do, but I love you too. Always."

He hugged her lazily, knowing he'd have endless opportunities to do so in the future. "Hey, how did you get here, anyway?"

"I drove! I was going down the highway, thinking about you. And I just didn't stop. I didn't let myself believe that I was actually going to drive all the way here until I stopped for gas about twenty miles outside of the city."

"You're crazy, you know that?" He kissed the top of her head, loving the feel of her silky hair against his cheek.

"My parents thought so, too, when I called them from the gas station! But I think they understood."

"You must have pretty cool parents."

Meg nodded. "I do. Which you'll find out when you meet them."

As Tim studied Meg's face he thought of the promise he'd made to himself on the airplane. *I'm going to be completely honest,* he'd sworn. "Meg, before we talk about anything else, there's a bunch of stuff I have to tell you—*want* to tell you."

She smiled and brushed the hair off his forehead. Tim took a deep breath and continued. "See, it doesn't really have anything to do with you and me, but then again, it does." He stopped. *I sound like a babbling idiot,* he thought. "Anyway, her name was Melinda, and she—"

"Tim, you don't need to tell me," Meg interrupted.

"No, I want to. Really. I don't want any more secrets between us."

"Ollie told me all about it. All about you and Melinda, I mean."

Tim was dumbfounded. "Everything? Even the part about her staying over in my dorm room?"

Meg nodded. "Yep. And it's all okay. What's past is past."

"Wait a second. Why were you talking to Ollie?"

"I went to see him at Lakesmith Hall a few days ago."

"Really? Why?" He could just imagine the wonderful impression Ollie must have made on Meg.

She moved farther into the room. "Well, I was driving down the highway that day, too, thinking about you. I missed you so much, I almost kept driving straight on to D.C. right then." She paused.

"But?" he prompted.

"But I didn't have the nerve. I figured you'd probably slam the door in my face."

"Never happen." He shook his head.

Meg smiled and gave him a quick hug. "I know that—now. Anyway, I was so desperate to at least talk about you and find out what you were doing that I turned my car around and drove to Lakesmith. I found Ollie, and the rest, as they say, is history."

"Wow! He must have been surprised to see you."

"He took it in stride. Even the part where I started crying like a baby. He's a great guy. In fact, if Gretchen didn't already have a boyfriend . . ."

"So while you were crying he filled you in on my whole sordid past?"

Meg nodded. "Something like that. Then he convinced me that you still loved me." She put her arms around Tim's waist and smiled up at him. "To make a long story short, here I am."

Tim shook his head. "I guess I owe him one. Even if he did spill my guts."

"Let's think about how we can thank him later. Right now . . ."

"What?"

"I need a kiss!"

Saying thanks to Oliver was the last thing on Tim's mind as he leaned forward to oblige Meg. "For you, ma'am, I've got a million." He stared into her big brown eyes. "And all the time in the world."

The Truth About Love is Elizabeth Winfrey's first novel for young adults. Ms. Winfrey comes from Kansas City, but she currently lives in New York's Greenwich Village, where she writes and edits. She recently graduated from Columbia University. She would never, ever lie to her boyfriend.

$1,000.00

FOR YOUR THOUGHTS

Let us know what you think. Just answer these seven questions and you could win $1,000! For completing and returning this survey, you'll be entered into a drawing to win a $1,000 prize.

OFFICIAL RULES: *No additional purchase necessary.* Complete the HarperPaperbacks questionnaire—be sure to include your name and address—and mail it, with first-class postage, to HarperPaperbacks, Survey Sweeps, 10 E. 53rd Street, New York, NY 10022. Entries must be received no later than midnight, October 4, 1995. One winner will be chosen at random from the completed readership surveys received by HarperPaperbacks. A random drawing will take place in the offices of HarperPaperbacks on or about October 16, 1995. The odds of winning are determined by the number of entries received. If you are the winner, you will be notified by certified mail how to collect the $1,000 and will be required to sign an affidavit of eligibility within 21 days of notification. A $1,000 money order will be given to the *sole winner* only—to be sent by registered mail. Payment of any taxes imposed on the prize winner will be the sole responsibility of the winner. All federal, state, and local laws apply. Void where prohibited by law. The prize is not transferable. **No photocopied entries.**

Entrants are responsible for mailing the completed readership survey to HarperPaperbacks, Survey Sweeps, at 10 E. 53rd Street, New York, NY 10022. If you wish to send a survey without entering the sweepstakes drawing, simply leave the name/address section blank. Surveys without name and address will not be entered in the sweepstakes drawing. HarperPaperbacks is not responsible for lost or misdirected mail. Photocopied submissions will be disqualified. Entrants must be at least 18 years of age and U.S. citizens. All information supplied is subject to verification. Employees, and their immediate family, of HarperCollins*Publishers* are not eligible. For winner information, send a stamped, self-addressed Nº10 envelope by November 10, 1995 to HarperPaperbacks, Sweeps Winners, 10 E. 53rd Street, New York, NY 10022.